It's beignets versus ___ and her loyal gofer Henrietta ("Henny" to her friends) cross ladies over the contents of a planned cookbook. What follows is a nicely convoluted murder mystery and a glorification of America's diverse cuisines, played out against the attractions of a lovingly drawn Chicago.

—Fred Erisman, *In Their Own Words: Forgotten Women Pilots of Early Aviation.*

You'll find yourself cheering for Henny James as she works beyond her job description as prep assistant to save her boss, Irene Foxglove, glamorous local French-ish TV chef, from dangers that lurk behind the scenes, plunging them into a complicated hot stew, boiling over with trouble, not only for them, but for Irene's family and Henny's delicious (but gay) neighbor, Patrick. Henny needs to figure this out quick, before her goose is cooked.

—Kaye George, *Deadly Sweet Tooth (Vintage Sweets Mysteries Book 2)*

In this fun new read, Henny James finds herself in hot water just trying to do her job as a prep chef for Irene Foxglove's television cooking show. If her boss's name sounds poisonous, you can be sure something even more dangerous is going on. Henny has to improvise a recipe to discover the secret before someone else—or Henny herself—dips into a deadly dish and is harmed.

—Edith Mawell/Maddie Day, Agatha Award-winning author of *Nacho Average Murder in the Country Store Mysteries*

Saving Irene is a really good cozy mystery—hard to put down and stays with you. Pick up *Saving Irene* and get lost in the beauty of Chicago and the intrigue of a Texas girl making her way in the world while protecting a snooty not-quite-famous television chef and cultivating a friendship with an out-of-reach Adonis of a neighbor. You won't see the end coming.

—Mary Dulle, an avid reader and Judy Alter fan

Saving Irene

A Culinary Mystery

By Judy Alter

Saving Irene

by Judy Alter

Alter Ego Press

Fort Worth, TX 76110-1233

ISBN 978-0-9969935-5-5 *(digital)*

ISBN 978-0-9969935-6-2 *(trade paperback)*

Editor: Lourdes Venard, Comma Sense Editing

Cover Art Design: Amy Balamut

Release Date: September 2020

With grateful thanks to Mary Dulle, reader extraordinaire, and Carol Roark, research guru. These ladies keep my writing honest.

Contents

Chapter One

At five foot nine, Irene Foxglove towers over me by a good five inches. This was particularly unpleasant when she was angry, and she was angry this day.

"Henrietta, the béchamel sauce is scorched." Those loud, slightly disdainful deep tones rang out like a bell.

I hate to be called by my proper name, Henrietta. When given such a last name as James, you'd think my mother would have chosen a matching simple first name, maybe Sue. But no, she chose Henrietta. When I was a kid, the other children teased me about having a boy's name and shortened it to Henny. Chef Irene Foxglove calls me Henrietta, and I cringe a bit half the time. She, on the other hand, prefers to be addressed as "Madame." Given my druthers, I'd address her as "Bitch." But I work for her—and today, Madame was displeased.

Irene has a low-budget, local TV cooking show, from a small independent Chicago production company and cleverly titled *Cooking with Irene,* on an independent station. I am her gofer. It's not a glamorous job, but when your eye is on a career in television, you start where you can. My goal in life is to be a producer, doing documentaries. International cuisines intrigue me—I read a lot of Anthony Bourdain—but so does American cooking. Meanwhile, as her "culinary assistant"—my grand title—it's my responsibility to assemble and prepare all ingredients before the shoot, so Irene looks organized and skillful. I'm not just behind the scenes. During a shoot, I have to wear a white butcher's apron—but no chef's hat like Irene—because I occasionally have to walk onto the set to hand her something.

I've learned to squelch my natural instincts to be a smart mouth and instead to be accommodating, so rather than "Make it yourself," I said, "I'll fix it." How in heaven's name can you scorch béchamel sauce? It's nothing but the white sauce my mom taught me to make dressed up with a bit of nutmeg. But I took the pan, cleaned it, and made a new batch of sauce that passed muster.

Then she looked at the menu for the day, the one that would show onscreen for viewers, and literally shrieked. "Henrietta! The béchamel has no accent mark. It cannot go like this. We will appear as provincial bumpkins." In Madame's mind nothing could be more damning than the provincial label. I fixed that too. I was her fixer.

Today's dish was croque monsieur or, if want to put it in plain English, a grilled ham-and-cheese. The béchamel, sometimes called the mother of French sauces, was used to slather the inside of the ham-and-gruyere concoction. Irene was ticking off the ingredients, checking to be sure I had them all ready and measured. Butter? Flour? Nutmeg? Sliced ham—is it the very best you could get? And so it went. I had it all laid out in neat little glass ramekins. After making the basic sandwich, Irene would top if off with a fried egg, transforming it instantly into a croque madame. I didn't have a Texas name for that—we didn't often top a grilled cheese with a fried egg back home.

"I guess we're ready." She said this with a certain reluctance, and I thought she was probably tired. It was a late afternoon shoot—for economy's sake, we shoot when no one else is using the studio. The production company, which has to pay for studio time and crew, decreed that it would be that way, which meant we often shot in the evening or on weekends. To maintain a weekly show with some comfortable backlog, we tried to shoot twice a week. The rest of the time was spent planning our upcoming menus and shows. For planning sessions, I had to trek from Hyde Park on Chicago's South Side to the North Shore, where Irene lived. And then there were the hours I spent in my apartment kitchen, searching out recipes that would please Madame, trying them, and frequently pre-preparing a dish for the next shoot.

We never saw anyone from Great Lakes Production. Howard Foxglove, Irene's doting husband, acted as their spokesperson or liaison or whatever. Sometimes I thought Howard was anonymously the CEO of Great Lakes, because he handed me a paycheck, gave me the credit card for groceries, and handled any problems that came up in the studios. He was the one, for instance, who negotiated a second cameraman so that Irene could be viewed from a variety of angles.

Low-budget also applied to Legacy Studios. Nothing was fancy, and Irene had at first railed against the kitchen setup, with a standard oven, a gas cooktop, utilitarian chrome work surface, and cutting boards that could be scrubbed for sanitation. Irene scorned such gadgets as instant pots and air fryers, so the counters were clean and neat. There was a microwave, because sometimes you just have to use it.

Irene could be arrogant and demanding one minute, charming the next. She was knowledgeable but pretended to be just enough humble or shy that viewers, uncertain of their own cooking skills, identified with her. She wore her dark hair swept neatly back into an old-fashioned chignon, except for a few tendrils that escaped and softened the look. Before a shoot, a woman, no doubt hired by Howard, did Irene's makeup, hair, and nails. Those nails, on camera on close-up shots, had to be perfect.

I, on the other hand, stumbled onto the set looking as if I'd just wandered in—the morning's careful brushing of my long, blond hair having fallen victim to the pace of work and the breezes of fans that kept the studio from being stuffy. Too often, I had a splotch of this or that on my apron. And my nails? Let's just not talk about that. I've never had a manicure in my life.

This day, Irene wore a turquoise top of some kind under her coverall white apron and had a chef's hat perched on her head. She wasn't yet fifty, I was sure of that, and yet she had the air of self-assurance that usually comes only with age. Lord knows, I was a long way from having it.

My long-sleeved T-shirt was a dark brown, so that it wouldn't clash with Irene's outfit. She always called me before a shoot, so that we could coordinate. Make that so that I could coordinate my outfit to whatever she had chosen to wear. Much as I would have loved to wear jeans to work, Irene had a thing against denim. I often wore chinos—my compromise.

About her toque. When I asked, as a new employee, where she took her culinary training, she eyed me for a long moment, then waved a hand airily and said, "France. Of course, France." I wondered if the truth was something like Kendall College in Chicago. But she was all about France—French recipes, as today demonstrated, French phrases that she dropped here and there, even what she thought of as a French fashion style, chignon and all.

My doubts about her training came because sometimes I had to give her small cooking hints, things mostly my mother had taught me: a pinch of sugar in tomato-based sauces, which led Irene to say, "Mais oui, that is what we did in France." Or a few drops of olive oil to keep pasta from clumping while you put finishing touches on the sauce. She'd say, "Good for the home cook, no? The chef, not so much. Not needed." I wanted to reply that pasta is pasta, and it is all starch, and it will get gummy.

The shoot that afternoon was hard. When she was stressed, Irene had a tremor in her left hand, and today it was back. I had no idea what particular stress was causing it, nor did I want to ask. When she spilled the flour, I quickly measured out some more and ran it in to her. She filled the time by chatting on about the difficulty of getting béchamel just right. Which she almost didn't do if she thought it was scorched. I supposed the film crew wouldn't mind as much as I did. They were the ones who would eat it. Irene nearly burnt the outside of the sandwich because her timing was off, but it was cooked onscreen and there was nothing I could do about it.

Obviously flustered, she chattered on about how to pace your cooking so that the meal was all ready at once. And finally, she broke the egg yolk on her first try at transferring the fried egg from skillet to sandwich. Wordlessly, I handed her another egg.

Irene Foxglove was clearly off her game, and I worried that something more than fatigue was bothering her. Easy as she was to resent, Irene still struck a chord of sympathy in me. She was wound tight in the way that only insecure people are. I'd catch her staring off into space, and when I gently tried to bring her back to reality, she'd look around for a moment, startled, as though she couldn't remember where she was.

Once I accidentally found her in a small anteroom off the kitchen, crumpled-up paper clutched in her fist, tears running down her face, carrying mascara and makeup with them. My first thought was that I hoped the cosmetician was still around. My second, more logical one was, *What could have reduced the elegant, self-assured Madame to tears?* Later, I found a useless clue—a photo nearly swept out of sight under a cabinet. A tall, young man held an infant, maybe a year old with a halo of golden curls around her head. I didn't think the man was Howard Foxglove, but I was certain that the child was the daughter Irene doted on, Gabrielle Foxglove, now nineteen years old and spoiled rotten. In my mind, the more Irene catered to that girl, the more the child demanded—and was scornful of her mother, defiant to Howard. No secret that I didn't like Gabrielle.

By the time we reconvened in the kitchen that day, Irene's makeup and her self-confidence had been restored, and she never missed a beat, never mentioned the incident. I knew not to ask.

But Irene almost never had days when she was as off her game as this day. Finally, the director said those blessed words, "It's a wrap." It was nine o'clock.

* * *

Howard Foxglove came quietly into the studio, as we were gathering up our things, and the cleaning crew prepared to mop up all that spilled flour and shattered glass. Tall as his wife and as fair as she is dark, he is a gentle, quiet man who was, I thought, completely mesmerized by the woman he'd married. He dutifully leaned in to kiss her cheek and murmur something soft in French.

With a secretive smile, she responded in French, so I was totally left out of the conversation. This wasn't unusual. They often spoke French to each other. It reminded me of my mother and her sister, who spoke pig Latin to each other when they didn't want us kids to know what they were saying. I had noticed that Irene and Howard frequently spoke in French in the presence of Gabrielle.

"You don't know the half of it." She tried to make it a joke but failed, and for just a flickering moment there, she clung to her husband, revealing that usually hidden vulnerable side to my boss.

Howard patted her back, as he would a child, and asked, "Berghoff's?"

She sighed. "I don't think I could do heavy German so late at night. Morton's for a steak?" The truth was that Madame found German food inferior. I found that out the first time I suggested a sausage and kraut menu.

"Of course, my dear." But he blanched just a bit. "Perhaps we can split something."

"I'll just run and powder my nose," she said. "Won't be a minute." And she disappeared into the inner part of the studio, leaving me alone with Howard. We rarely spoke, but not out of antipathy. We just didn't have much to say to each other.

The thing I always noticed about Howard was that he had no chin. All those clichés about weak-chinned men went through my mind every time I looked at him. He was good-looking, in a very British sort of way. It was rumored that he was descended from the English peerage, and I supposed he could be a twenty-first century version of the second son, sent to America to find his fortune. Was Foxglove a name from the landed gentry? It was ironic that a chef married a man whose last name was synonymous with a poisonous plant.

As for being a second son, Howard seemed to have found his fortune already, for they lived lavishly—I couldn't afford Morton's once a year if I wanted to. I knew Irene didn't make the money from a weekly local show to support their lifestyle. And yet that line about splitting a steak—was Howard suddenly worried about money? I had no idea what the man did while Irene and I were working long days. I doubted he had a mistress on the side, but he could have been sitting in on high stakes poker or playing the horses. Or he could have been a stockbroker or an accountant in a dull old office.

I sent them on their way to Morton's and crawled into my car. I'd duck into Harper Foods to find a dinner in a bag with my name practically written on it—beef bourguignon, thyme-baked potatoes, and green beans almondine. Enough leftovers I might just hunker down and not leave the apartment at all tomorrow. I know, I know, isolation is not good for the soul, but there are times your own company is best.

Chapter Two

My dream of leftovers faded quickly when Patrick, my neighbor next door, knocked on my door. I met Patrick O'Malley ten months ago when I moved in. Unpacking, wearing torn jeans (not the fashionable kind), and a Tri Delt sweatshirt, I knew I looked a mess. It was hot, and unpacking is hot work, the kind that pulls your hair out of that messy ponytail you stuck it into and smears whatever makeup was left on from last night.

Patrick, however, did not look a mess. Despite his oh-so-Irish name, he did not have the proverbial map of Ireland on his face. Hollywood screenwriters would have called his features chiseled, his nose aquiline but without the usual bump, his eyes as blue-green as the waters of the Caribbean—oops, I'm getting carried away. I've never seen those blue-green waters. But I knew the package standing before me was good-looking. Probably six inches taller than me and four or five years older than my twenty-five, he looked like he ran four times a week and lifted weights the other three days. His hair was medium dark and medium long, with one piece that kept creeping onto his forehead until he brushed it back impatiently. I was immediately convinced he was gay—you know, that old too-good-to-be-true theory.

In his hand, he held a measuring cup. I riveted my attention on it so I could stop staring at him.

With a grin, he said, "I came to borrow a cup of sugar. Isn't that how you meet your new neighbor?"

"But," I managed to reply, "I'm the newcomer. I'm supposed to ask you for the sugar."

"Yeah, but I bet you don't know where a measuring cup is." With laughing eyes, he took in the mess behind me—boxes half unpacked, dishes and groceries stacked and nearly falling off the counters, clothes thrown on the couch. "Want some help?"

I'm no shrinking violet. I accepted his offer. We began with the kitchen. Since cooking is where my head is these days, I knew exactly how I wanted it arranged, and he followed directions perfectly, laughing at me for being compulsive.

We made the bed together without any innuendo, further cementing my instinct about his sexual preferences, and hung my clothes in the bigger-than-I-expected closet, neatly arranged into summer, in-between, and winter. We unpacked the boxes of books I couldn't leave behind, and he expertly assembled the Ikea bookcase I'd bought.

While we worked, we talked. I told him how upset my family was that I was leaving Texas for Chicago because of a TV job. "There are TV stations in Houston and Dallas," my mom had protested. But after being jilted two weeks before my wedding by a football/frat boy hero type, I was ready to fly. And Chicago beckoned. I read about the city until I decided on the Hyde Park neighborhood because it sounded funky and interesting and a far cry from suburbia, where I'd grown up and the sort of unreal world of college. I played blind man's bluff with realtors, chose one, dickered with her over the phone, and sight unseen, rented my apartment. Then I loaded my Honda, gently wriggled out from under Mom's insistence she come with me, and drove from Texas to Chicago.

Perched on the third floor of an older apartment building on Cornell Avenue, just south of Fifty-Fifth Street, my new home was a one-bedroom and a large living-kitchen combination. I could cook, read, and write all in the same cheery space. The kitchen area showed evidence of sporadic updating but never renovation. Linoleum floor, only slightly scuffed, and Formica countertops, and, praise be, a four-burner gas stove, almost old enough to be vintage. The rest of the apartment had hardwood floors and woodwork that was stained dark. Three windows in a bay in the living room looked out on a street of trees and red brick buildings, except the one next door had slate towers that reminded me of a castle.

Patrick's apartment was in the back of the building and so lacked my bay window with its fantasy-inducing view of the towers next door. Otherwise, it was pretty similar, except that it's so full of loaded bookshelves that I swear the floors will collapse someday.

Patrick is a post-doc fellow at the University of Chicago, working in observational astrophysics—he had to explain that observational astrophysics basically meant studying the skies, recording data, and trying to figure out what it meant for human life. "I can show you the stars," he said with a poor attempt at a leer, and I knew he didn't mean it that way. Nor did I take it. He also played the clarinet, which he said relaxed him. I'd learned to listen for his music sometimes when I came home late at night to a quiet building.

Career plans? The question made him stare out the window. Finally, he said, "Government, I suppose. An agency involved with mission planning. I'll never be an astronaut, but someday going into space won't be that tough. More people will be able to go without the rigorous training the pioneers have undergone. I want to be on one of those trips."

I felt as if I were watching him take off on a rocket ship, and I shivered involuntarily. His next question drew me back to the present moment.

"What about you?"

"Cooking," I replied. It didn't sound at all glamorous compared to his life plans, so I hurried on before he could ask about husband and babies and was that my only ambition. "On television." It was my turn to think for a long minute. "I guess my dream job would be to coordinate the cooking segments on the *Today* show." I'm sure,

looking back, that I made it clear that I was through with men—
forever. Once burned, twice shy, that sort of thing.

He ignored that protest and jumped right ahead to the future.
"You'll be in New York, and I'll be in Houston. We can email."

"By then, there will be more sophisticated ways of keeping in
touch," I predicted loftily. "Commuter spaceships and the like."

"I'll work on it," he promised. "Where's home?"

"Texas. Just outside Fort Worth, sort of a suburb that's really
just a development. My dad's an accountant—not a CPA, just an
accountant in a bank." *Why did I always have to add that and dimin-
ish my poor sweet father who, I think, was relieved when he thought I
was about to give up this television foolishness and get married, give
him grandbabies, and limit my cooking to a family.* "Mom taught high
school home ec—and taught me to cook."

"And do you?" he asked. "I mean cook. Can I look forward to
some neighborly meals?"

I smiled. It would be nice to have a buddy. "Yeah, I like to cook. You?"

He was modest. "I cook a bit too." It turned out, among other
things, he made killer spaghetti sauce and chili that rivaled any I'd
had in Texas. And there was no way I could fix him any good Texas
barbecue. Maybe I'd wow him with chicken-fried steak.

I told him about my two sisters—Janie, two years older, and
Ellie, three years behind me, and how close I was to them and that
I missed them already.

"Maybe they'll come visit. I like having pretty women around."
He grinned self-consciously, and I thought how like a gay man that
was. Any that I'd known had loved having women around—they
just didn't want to do anything about it.

"They probably will be here so often you'll get tired of them," I
said absently.

That evening, Patrick offered to take me to a nearby Mediter-
ranean restaurant. I showered, washed and dried my hair, and let
it hang about my shoulders. I wore a casual long dress of light blue
cotton and matching strappy sandals, the sort of look that took me
back to my Austin days. And I took unusual care with my makeup.
Okay, so he's gay. He could have friends.

"You clean up nicely," he said.

We ate falafel and baba ghanoush and tzatziki with pita triangles, meatballs, and dolma, and incongruous caramel chocolate cake for dessert, which we ate with our fingers and got all sticky. I envisioned a lifetime platonic friendship beginning that night and wondered why I dreamt of the guy who'd jilted me. He'd shrunk in size and aged poorly.

In no time, Patrick became my best friend, the person I needed in my life. I missed my sisters—telephone calls only go so far, and my girlfriends from high school were beyond me, most married and talking about babies while they worked daily jobs. My college sorority sisters had moved on to more exciting lives and careers—law school, one to work for a private investigator's firm, another to banking investments. When I emailed those girls, I played up the glamorous aspects of my TV work, which sometimes amounted to writing a novel since a lot of imagination went into those descriptions. But I no longer had a bestie, someone with whom I could share my every thought.

Patrick became my bestie. It was uncomplicated and easy because there was none of that physical stuff—will he kiss me? Does he expect me to sleep with him? Shoot, Patrick didn't even hold my hand. Oh, he'd take my elbow to guide me down some steps or give me a friendly hug sometimes, but that was it.

We went to movies, we ate at small restaurants in Hyde Park, where he seemed to know everyone. We went on bike rides, and he told me all about the Midway, that green strip that runs by the university from Jackson Park to the lake. It was once, he said, the sight of the Columbian Exposition, where countries from all over the world built sparking white palaces to show off their accomplishments, from agriculture and women's crafts to science and technology. And then there was the actual Midway, where Buffalo Bill had his Wild West, Egyptian belly dancers horrified proper society matrons, and George Washington Ferris built his giant wheel. Patrick told it all with such enthusiasm that I wanted to travel back in time, to be part of it, to ride that Ferris wheel.

I laughed at him when we wandered through the massive Museum of Science and Industry. He refused to go down into the coal mine, saying his sights were set on the stars, not under the ground.

All those straight friends I thought he'd have? Never met a one of them. Not gay ones either. Every once in a while, he'd mention a fraternity brother or a cousin he was close to, but he didn't seem to miss male companionship, maybe because he was an only child and never had that really close companionship. We ate dinner together three or four nights a week, called each other in moments of high celebration and dark despair, and pretty much shared our lives.

The night I crept home to drown myself in beef bourguignon, he walked in and headed for the kitchen. Spying the brown bag with my dinner, he said, "What did you bring us tonight?" Before I could answer he was pulling out containers, reading the labels, and shouting, "My favorite! How did you know that's just what I wanted tonight?"

I was almost grumpy. "Because I need cheering?"

"What's wrong in the land of television food?"

I could tell he didn't take me seriously, and in retrospect it seemed a bit silly. So Irene had an off night, and Howard seemed suddenly penurious? I was probably reading too much into nothing. I shrugged.

"We need a movie," he said. "I'm even up for a chick flick to cheer you."

We watched *Same Kind of Different as Me* and ate my beef bourguignon sitting cross-legged on my floor. I felt more cheerful.

Chapter Three

Sundays became Mom's night to call and check on me. This particular night she wanted to know if I'd made any friends. Had I gone to a church where I might meet some nice young people?

"No, Mom, not yet. But there's a guy who has the apartment next to me. We're becoming friends."

"Well," she said philosophically, "don't reel in the first fish that takes your bait. See what else is in the water."

And Mom doesn't even fish! She was right, but so far, I hadn't missed people my age. I had Patrick for company, and Irene was keeping me too busy for a social life. When I wasn't with her planning meals or taping shows, I was sitting up at night poring over food magazines, studying cookbooks, searching for inspiration. And trying to improve my skills. The idea of culinary school lingered in the back of my mind, but for now I was busy and happy.

* * *

Monday morning. Irene welcomed me into their Clarendon Avenue apartment on the North Side with what I took as a warning. "Penny's joining us this morning. I'm afraid we won't get much menu planning done. She is super excited about some new plan she has to rocket me to stardom in the TV culinary world." Irene's artificial laugh told me she wasn't really laughing off the possibility.

Penny Aldrich is Irene's publicist, an inappropriately named square block of a woman of indeterminate age with gray hair cut as square as her shape. She dresses in mannish suits, carries a huge briefcase everywhere she goes, and is supposed to be "fabulous" at what she does.

As an afterthought, Irene added, "I've asked Howard to sit in with us." Translation: this is going to cost Howard money, and he best hear about it firsthand. At least that sort of solved my curiosity about what Howard did during the day. It was nothing he couldn't rearrange to suit his wife's needs.

The Foxglove apartment may not have a lake view, though you can see it in the distance if you look hard. But it has the lovely green Clarendon Park right in front of it, and it's on a street of mansions, many now converted to apartments. Built in the early 1900s, Irene's building is three stories of red brick with intense green trim, lots of it. Sort of like a Christmas tree all year around.

Irene and her family live on the second floor in what appeared to be half the building. A huge apartment that I was told had three bedrooms, though I had never seen them. I did see a bright sunroom that looked out on the park and would, I knew, be a perfect spot for curling up with a book on a chaise. The apartment reflects Irene's effort to please her husband—it's masculine and British to the point that it reminded me of the old and exclusive men's clubs we now see only in movies—overstuffed leather chairs, leather-topped end tables, chintz in the sunroom. Oriental rugs covering the polished oak floors. All amazingly comfortable and homey. Compared to many contemporary decors, this apartment made you want to settle down, sink in, and make yourself comfortable.

The extravagantly long dining table bore a gleaming dark finish, and every time I sat at it for our planning sessions, I wondered if it was mahogany. Today, four places were set at one end, with a pitcher of juice, a coffeepot, cups and glasses, and a basket of croissants.

Just as the door chime announced Penny, Howard slipped into the dining room in his usual unobtrusive way. For the first time in my knowledge of him, he was wearing soft chino pants and a J.Crew pullover. We greeted each other and sat silent across the table, eyes wandering, with nothing to say for each other. We waited for Irene to fetch Penny.

The publicist seemed to blow into the room, slamming her briefcase on that beautiful table with a certain brusqueness. Her suit this day was gunmetal gray, softened only slightly by a pink scarf. She nodded at Howard and then me but favored us with no more greeting than that. Uninvited, she took the armchair at the head of the table, poured herself coffee, and announced, "Wait till you hear what I have in mind."

We were not so breathless as to pass up coffee and croissants. Her words served as a signal to dig in. But once we were settled with our food, Penny looked directly at Irene and said, "You're going to publish a cookbook." It was not a question or a suggestion; it was a command, to which Irene responded incredulously, "I am?"

Right there, at that moment, I knew who would get the bulk of the work, but I said nothing. Howard too remained silent, but I thought I detected wariness beneath his usual bland façade, and, for a moment, I warmed to him.

Penny charged on. "I've thought of titles. First, we have to decide how many recipes. Initially I thought fifty, but perhaps that's too many. What about a book called *Irene's Favorite Forty?*"

I didn't point out that most cookbooks had far more than forty recipes.

Irene gulped. "I guess I have forty recipes. I particularly like, for instance, that croque monsieur we did the other day, and of course my Coquilles St.-Jacques. And there's that molasses and soy glaze for salmon . . . " Her voice trailed off, and I squelched the urge to say encouragingly, "Great. Only thirty-seven to go."

"Think about this," Penny went on, pencil in hand, making furious notes of what? Ideas as they popped into her fertile brain. "Do you want a book that cooks will use or one of those beautiful coffee-table books that everyone raves about, but no one cooks from."

"Well, I've always wanted to share my recipes with others," Irene began, only to be interrupted by Howard.

"Have you done a profit statement on this project?" he asked softly. Fingers twirling a pencil gave away the inner turmoil his soft voice hid. "Initial cost? Expected returns. What expenses are to be incurred, including marketing."

Penny waved a hand in the air, virtually dismissing such a boring topic. "We'll get to all that."

Talk went on for two hours, while I squirmed and willed myself to keep my mouth shut. There were times I could have jumped in. Having been on the yearbook staff in high school and worked in a bookstore my college summers I knew just enough to put the dampness of reality onto Penny's great plans. But I didn't.

Lunchtime came, and Howard offered to send out for sandwiches from a nearby deli, but Penny declined. She had, she said, "other fish to fry. You just stay here and begin planning." Then she threw a bone to Howard. "When we have a plan, like how big a book, what size, all those details, we'll start gathering costs, thinking about pricing and marketing. Of course, we'll have to have full color and a food photographer." And she breezed out, her exit as abrupt as her entrance had been.

And there we sat, facing chicken salad on croissants, with blank legal pads in front of each of us. Well, mine was not quite blank: it said, in list form, "Croque Monsieur, Coquille St.-Jacques, Molasses-Soy Glazed Salmon." Every big project must start somewhere.

"I'm overwhelmed," Irene said. "I think I'll take some aspirin. In fact, I think I'll lie down with a wet rag on my head." She did look a bit pale.

Figuring I was no longer needed, I gathered up my legal pad and my purse, but Howard put out a gentle hand and stopped me. "Stay. I'd like some company while I eat my lunch, and there's no sense wasting your sandwich. I'll just wrap Irene's and put it up for later. She'll recover faster than either of us expect."

This sudden expression of humanity from Howard, whom I always dismissed as bland, startled me so that I almost jumped. But I saw an intense expression in his eyes, almost a pleading, and I sat down, muttering a phrase my mother had long tried to get me to use, "It would be my pleasure."

"Good." In one graceful movement, he scooped up Irene's sandwich and disappeared into the kitchen, while I sat trying to think of things to talk to Howard about.

I had no need of planned topics. Howard had something on his mind. He returned almost instantly, carrying two glasses of white wine. "Here's to a best-selling cookbook," he said, touching his glass lightly to mine. Then he sat down, lifted his sandwich, paused, and said, "I want this cookbook to be a success, perfect in every way. I want that for Irene, but I will have to rely on you." With that he took a bite of his sandwich.

With my mouth full, I could only nod. Finally, I managed, "I'll do whatever I can. But Irene has recipes and good taste. She won't need my help." The wine was crisp and good. Even with my unsophisticated palate, I could detect hints of peach and lemon.

"No," Howard said slowly, putting down his sandwich. "She will. Irene can be—ah, difficult." He looked as though it pained him to say that. "And Penny is Hitler in drag."

The phrase startled me, so I almost hooted aloud, but I managed to restrain myself and utter, "I think I see what you mean."

"They're bound to clash," Howard said, "and it could get ugly. You will have to mediate." He took another measured bite. "Steer Penny away from extravagance. And help Irene learn what realistically should be in a cookbook. Forty isn't many recipes."

Even as I said, "No, it's not enough," I was thinking, *Me? A peacemaker? Curb Penny's budget?* None of that was in my job description, and at the moment I itched to be gone from this lavish apartment, to run home to safety and Patrick. But at the rate Howard was devouring his sandwich, we were liable to be at this table until suppertime.

Speaking softly, Howard went on, "I worry about Irene's emotional health, of course. But I also worry about her physical safety."

Irene in danger? I wanted to laugh and protest and—could he be right? What kind of danger could Irene be in? Worst I could think of was a grease burn from carelessness on the set.

Just as I said, "Howard, you can't be serious," he said, "There has been a threat—"

A whiny female voice interrupted him. "Lunch without me?" Gabrielle Foxglove strolled languidly into the dining room. "Where's Mother?"

Howard, who always stood when a woman came into the room, remained seated and replied calmly, "Your sandwich is in the fridge with your name on it. And your mother is not feeling well. She's gone to lie down. Please don't disturb her."

Almost as tall as her mother, Gabrielle was as fair as Irene was dark, but she had her mother's thin shape and almost regal posture. In other words, she moved and acted like the self-indulgent princess that she was. There seemed to be little of Howard in her, certainly not the gentle spirit. Perhaps the fair coloring.

Today Gabrielle wore torn jeans, the expensive kind where the tears are designer dictated, strappy spike sandals, and a voluminous beige top that accented her golden hair. No makeup, and her hair hung loose around her face, causing her to occasionally brush it out of her eyes.

"Sorry, *Father,* but I have to talk to her immediately." And with that, she hurried off toward the bedroom wing of the apartment.

Howard looked grim and pushed his sandwich away, as though after two bites he was through eating. I was too on edge to take another bite—thanks goodness I had almost finished the sandwich. I waited for Howard to explain the threat, but he was silent, posed as though listening. In a moment I knew why. Loud, raised voices hit us, coming from the bedroom area. Irene and Gabrielle were shouting at each other. I couldn't make out the words, just the tone and the anger, and I thought neither was good for Irene's headache.

Howard listened for a moment and then rose, calmly picking up his plate and glass. "Shall we remove to the sunroom? It would put us a little more distant from the noise and we can talk privately."

I picked up my things and followed him, stunned into a silence unusual for me. As we left the dining room, I thought I heard Gabrielle threaten, "You have to tell me, or I'll ruin your show, your career, your life."

Howard led the way, and we settled in overstuffed chairs in front of the windows that looked out on Clarendon Park. To my amazement, he began to eat again. My sandwich gone, I sipped my wine and found my tongue.

"What's going on, Howard? What kind of a threat? Is Gabrielle the reason you're worried about Irene?"

"I doubt Gabrielle would ever hurt her mother. It's much more involved than that, but it's a family matter that I don't feel inclined to discuss right now. Suffice to say, I received a note threatening Irene's life. It . . . ah . . . upset me."

That better be putting it mildly! "Did you share it with Irene?"

He looked horrified for a moment. "No, of course not. I wouldn't want to upset her. You of all people know how delicate she is."

I never thought of Irene as delicate. Easily upset, yes, but not delicate. Now did not seem the time to say so. "Did you call the police?" Seemed logical to me, but he gave me a look that was almost pity for my innocence.

"Of course not. I am not willing to make this public."

I swallowed the exasperated sigh that rose in my throat. "I think you have to tell her so she can protect herself. It's not fair to let her go around thinking everything is hunky-dory when it's not." The minute I spoke, I wished I could retract my words. Who was I to tell him how to handle his "delicate" wife?

Abruptly, he changed the subject. "Do you have a license to carry?"

It was such an out-of-the-blue question that I almost blurted out, "Carry what?" But my brain kicked into gear, and I said, "No. I'm opposed to guns."

He sighed. "So am I, but I just thought . . . well, never mind. Do you have any training in the martial arts?"

I was losing it. "No, I don't, Howard. I have pepper spray on my key ring and a panic button on my phone. But I didn't sign on to be a bodyguard. I'm a chef's assistant, a gofer, and I'm happy with that."

"Of course, I'll raise your pay if you take on extra responsibilities for protecting Irene," he said, ignoring my words about not being a bodyguard. He went on to explain the financing of the show, something I'd never understood in the months I worked there. Although my check came from Great Lakes Production, I was actually Howard's employee. As the principal of Great Lakes, he had a contract with

Legacy Studios for production of Irene's show. All expenses went through Howard's hands—my salary, Penny's fees, supplies, and the flat fee to the studio, which included equipment, cameramen, and I don't know what else. I'd keep it in mind next time I wanted to complain about something. I was curious but couldn't ask what else Great Lakes Production was involved in. Maybe Howard didn't play poker all day every day after all.

He had finally finished his sandwich and a second glass of wine and seemed to have said all he wanted to say. Long periods of silence were, at least for me, awkward.

I stretched and rose. "Time for me to go home, if I want to beat the rush." It was only two o'clock, well in advance of rush hour, but the line sounded good. "Please tell Irene I hope she feels better. I'll go home and think about cookbooks." I was tempted to add "and murder," but I bit my tongue. It was as if the threatening note had never been mentioned, but I knew it had—and I couldn't forget.

At that moment, we heard Gabrielle shout, "I'll find him, no matter what it takes!" and the front door slammed.

Wearily, Howard said, "Believe whatever you will" and then he rose and walked me to the front door, which he held open with great courtesy. "Thank you, Henny. I know I can rely on you." He did? How did he know that? I didn't.

I lingered in the hallway to give Gabrielle a good heard start. And then I ran to the bus stop. I hadn't yet gotten up the nerve to drive on the Outer Drive and so I faced an hour's bus ride each way every time I came to the Clarendon apartment.

Chapter Four

They say every girl should have a gay man in her life. I don't know who the "they" with all this wisdom are, but I've been hearing that since I was about sixteen. Gay men, contrary to what you would think, don't resent women—they love them. And they treat them with a gentle courtesy and kind consideration that we don't get from a lot of those testosterone-driven males. All that abstract philosophy wasn't on my mind that Monday afternoon as I rode the CTA bus through the Loop and all the way to Hyde Park. I just knew that Patrick would give me the kind of comfort and advice I needed as I tried to wrap my mind around Howard's fears for Irene. Sure, it would be easy to resent her, but not enough to kill her. A small voice inside me countered with, "Some people don't need much provocation." If Irene was in danger, how could I protect her? Shoot, get right to the point: how could I keep myself safe?

It was too early for Patrick to be home when I got to the apartment about three thirty, but I knocked on his door anyway. Nothing. I spent the rest of the afternoon listening for him to come home. He usually gave a couple of sharp raps on my door, a way of saying

"I'm here" before he went into his own apartment. Five o'clock came and went, and then six. Nothing.

I busied myself, sort of, with studying Irene's portfolio of recipes, trying to mark ones for the cookbook and ones to cook in the coming week. Irene's portfolio, as to be expected, leaned heavily on French traditional cooking, and I didn't think many American cooks took that kind of time in the kitchen these days, Julia Child or no. But my mind kept going back to the idea of Irene in danger. From who? What kind of danger? What in God's good name was I expected to do about it?

By seven, I lost all pride and texted Patrick. "Will you be home soon? I need to talk."

He replied promptly. He'd gotten into a pickup basketball game with some guys from his department. They'd just finished and were going to Piccolo Mondo on Fifty-Sixth Street for tapas. Some of the guys were bringing their wives and did I want to meet them?

And apparently be the only girl with a gay guy? No, I didn't want to meet them. I wanted Patrick to myself, to listen to my tale of woe, to console me. I pleaded a headache but asked him to know when he came home.

"Before ten," he wrote back.

Ten o'clock! How long did it take them to eat tapas and drink cheap wine? I'd be asleep. I consoled myself that at least I knew the truth about his straight friends: they were all married.

Of course, at ten—actually thirteen minutes before ten—I was wired, sitting in the living room, waiting for his knock. I managed not to throw myself at him wantonly when he came in. There was a slight weave and stumble in his step as he headed for the refrigerator, asking, "You got red wine?" He looked beat and smelled like he needed a shower—the combined effects of a basketball game on a warm night and too much red wine.

I was pissed that he'd been out having a jolly time, while I sat home stewing. Just before I exploded, I caught myself. *Henrietta James! Are you jealous of a gay man?*

Patrick made himself right at home, stretching out on the couch, his wine on the floor beside him. Looking at me with one eye, he said, "Okay, spill it. What's going on?" Not quite the invitation to confidentiality I'd been hoping for. "What happened with the temperamental chef today?"

"Her publicist decided she should write a cookbook."

"That's it?" He sat up and stared at me. "You've got your panties in a wad because someone wants your boss to write a cookbook? Sounds like a great idea to me."

Clearly, he didn't understand. I thought he should instantly see the pitfalls. "It's not a simple matter . . . not like recording a scientific observation." *There, take that!*

He hooted and paid no attention to what I'd intended as an insult on his research. "What's hard about putting together a collection of the recipes she already has? I mean that coquille thing you told me about a couple of days ago. There must be others."

Some days I thought it would be easy for me to dislike Patrick. This was one of them. Perhaps I should ask, "What's so hard about looking at the stars?" but I didn't. I could hardly unfriend him, since he lived next door. "There are cookbooks and cookbooks," I said, reaching for patience. "Usable ones, expensive ones, spiral-bound ones, and loose-leaf notebooks. Penny says it needs photographs—and a professional food photographer. Howard's worried about the cost, and I'm worried about how much extra work it will mean for me."

"Aha!" Now he was on his feet. At least he'd woken up to some extent. "That's it. You're afraid you'll do a whole lot of work and get no credit."

"It's not the credit," I insisted, "it's the work. It's having to babysit Irene." He still looked skeptical. "There's more. Howard is afraid someone is trying to kill Irene." Okay, I exaggerated the threat for effect, and I was already ashamed of myself. Or maybe I didn't exaggerate. Howard had said the note threatened Irene's life, and I'd been chewing on those words ever since. Part of what I realized as I stewed and waited for Patrick to come home was that Irene may be a bitch, but she was a person. She had her good side, sometimes, and if push came to shove, I would always go to her defense. I might not leap, but I would never abandon her.

Patrick stared hard at me for a long minute and then sat back down on the couch, hard enough that he grunted when he landed.

I thought I had at last really gotten his attention—until he laughed. I threw a sofa pillow at him, with more force than I intended. He ducked, and the pillow hit the lamp on the end table behind him, knocking it to the floor, where the bulb shattered. Patrick stopped laughing, but he still stared at me.

"You're serious, aren't you?"

I nodded.

Without another word, he went to the kitchen for the broom and dustpan. I sat and watched him clean up the mess and set the lamp back on the table. Then I went to the kitchen and brought him a new lightbulb. With order restored, he repeated his question.

"You're serious, aren't you?"

I couldn't resist. "Deadly." And then couldn't stop laughing. For a couple of minutes both of us had the uncontrollable giggles. Patrick sobered first. We didn't throw any more pillows.

"Howard wants you to protect her, which puts you in danger. Have I got this right?"

I nodded.

"Seems you're the only one he trusts, which is neat but not neat. That publicist woman?" He pushed his hair off his forehead with one impatient gesture.

"He despises her. He didn't exactly say that, but I think it's a question of finances—Howard's money—and not a lot of results from Penny. She's supposed to be great, but Irene is still a second-tier chef at best."

"The daughter?"

"She's apparently part of the problem. He tried hard to shield me from it, but I heard the two of them shouting at each other today."

"The two who?"

"Irene and Gabrielle. There's someone Gabrielle wants to find, and she needs her mother to tell her who it is, where he is, or something like that. Howard was obviously embarrassed and angry that I had to overhear all this."

A mischievous grin came over his face. "All you have to do is something treacherous that will convince Howard you're untrustworthy too. Then you're off the hook."

I was reaching for another pillow when he protested, "Just joking. I know you can't do that. And wouldn't." He stared into space, and I sat and waited for him to come up with the answer to all my problems. Unfortunately, he didn't. "I don't know what to tell you, how to help you, Henny. You'll just have to watch your back every time you're with her."

Comforting thought. *Thank you, Patrick O'Malley.*

He read the look on my face accurately. "Aw, come on, Henny, don't look at me that way. You know I'll do whatever I can to help you. I just don't know what that is right now." Ostentatiously, he looked at his watch. "Oh gosh, I got to go to bed. Teaching an early class tomorrow." And, with a brotherly soft punch to my shoulder, he was gone.

I sat and stewed. And then I lay awake in bed wondering who wanted to hurt Irene and why.

Howard called early the next morning, sounding weary. "Irene still isn't feeling well. In fact, I was up half the night with her. I don't think you should count on working today. I'll call again tonight, but don't you call. Let me call you when the time is right."

Now what did that mean? *When the time is right.*

I distracted myself by spending a good chunk of the day at 57th Street Books, prowling their shelves of cookbooks, taking a stack, and settling myself in a comfortable reading chair, finally returning that stack and taking another. Once I dug into the big section of cookbooks, I was amazed at the choice to be made. Penny had barely scratched the surface with her suggestion that we decide between usable and artsy. I was probably there four hours, and I learned a lot.

Many cookbooks rest on the fame of the chef behind them—James Beard, Bobby Flay, Ina Garten, Martha Stewart, and others. Clearly Irene wasn't in that category—yet. We, or at least Penny, hoped to use the cookbook to boost her up the popularity ladder. But a cookbook by Irene Foxglove had to have appeal beyond her name.

I pretty quickly ruled out ethnic cookbooks. Irene would insist on French, the way she clung to the fiction of her French training, and I figured Julia Child and Jacques Pépin, among others, had pretty well covered that topic. And Irene would never go for Italian—all that pasta!—and she disliked all foods Asian. I suspected the trick was to interest her in American cooking, but it would need a hook.

One-product cookbooks like bread, or dessert, or soup were out. She'd consider that mundane. And no to cooking appliances—she did grudgingly use a crockpot now and again but never an instant pot, popular as they are, and never air fryers, which she doesn't understand. I found a cast-iron skillet cookbook, but she would scorn that as common. Quick and easy wasn't in her vocabulary either—if it were, I wouldn't be doing all the prep work I did for each show. The shelves of the store were glutted with books catering to special diets—gluten-free, dairy-free, keto, vegan and vegetarian, whole grains.

So what would showcase our diva chef? I pretty much came to the conclusion that it would have to be an old-fashioned general-ist's cookbook, with emphasis on main dishes. And home cooking, though we'd have to phrase it differently. Something about being a TV chef at home flitted through my mind. I'd call Penny sometime when Irene was otherwise occupied.

With that accomplished, I began the process of re-shelving the last of the books, hoping I'd gotten them in the right order. I was stiff from sitting too long, and my back protested with every reach for an upper shelf. Store staff never even glanced at me as I left without making a purchase. They were used to people who camped out in their store.

To treat myself on the walk home I detoured to the Bonjour Café and Bakery on Fifty-Fifth Street and had a chai latte and a spinach quiche. Hmm. Quiche should go into the cookbook. I could see myself making endless lists of dishes that might have eye appeal. Simple without saying easy, tasty . . . this was not going to be easy.

When I got home, I was exhausted and fell asleep on the couch.

Patrick woke me up, letting himself into the apartment. "Ha," he crowed, "I need to tell Howard what a poor watchdog you are. You didn't even hear me come in."

Stretching and yawning, I said, "I was asleep. I am never asleep when Irene is around. Trust me on that one."

He plopped himself down on the couch next to me and said, "I was so worried about you that I went shopping today. Brought you something." He was so excited that his voice almost squeaked. With a flourish, he drew something out of the plastic bag he carried.

I found myself staring at a round, egg-shaped pink thing with a key ring at the narrow end.

"It's a personal alarm, Henny. I won't demonstrate because it's god-awful loud—the sales guy set it off for me, and I nearly ran out of the store. But all you do is pull this little pin, and all hell breaks loose. To stop it, just push the pin in."

I stared some more. If Irene, the possible killer, and I were alone, who would that call? "Umm, thanks."

"Here, I'll put your keys on it right now." He did, and then he said, "I can get you a ladies' stun gun, small. Looks like a cell phone. And it comes in pink, matches."

Oh, Patrick, I thought you knew me, understood me. I do not want a stun gun, especially a pink one.

He sat down next to me. "Henny, I'm not sure you like my gift."

"Oh, I do, Patrick, I do. It's just . . . well, I never thought of myself carrying a stun gun, pink or any other color. It's taking me a minute to adjust."

He sobered. "I understand. But you know, I realized this afternoon how important you are to me. I called and didn't get an answer and . . . it scared me. I think you should protect Irene, but what really matters to me is that you protect yourself." He stared at me with those hypnotic blue-green eyes.

Personal alarms and stun guns be darned. All I could think at that moment was, "Why is God so unfair? Why did he give gay genes to the most handsome, kindest man I've ever met?"

Chapter Five

By the next morning, Irene called to say she was feeling better. As my dear grandmother would have said, she was back at herself. Wishing I had the nerve to brave Outer Drive traffic in my car, I took the bus north, and we got in two solid days of work, mostly planning recipes for the show. We had decided that, for the cookbook, making a dish part of a menu would add to the appeal of the show. It would guide viewers toward a complete menu—main dish, sides, and dessert. Coq au vin was paired with a salad and crème brûlée for a French meal that delighted Irene—and, yes, she could tell folks how to do crème brûlée. For a purely American meal, we put smothered pork chops with mashed potatoes and green beans, with a fudge brownie for dessert.

As we worked, heads together at the dining table, I'd stop every once in a while to glance at Irene. Who would want to kill her? And why? Howard wasn't around, so I guessed he had already put me on bodyguard duty.

By Thursday evening, we had outlined four meals, written the onscreen directions, and roughed out the cookbook entries. I made a note to ask Howard about calling a professional food photographer.

Irene saw my note and snapped, "Don't ask Howard. Just have someone—someone good—in the studio next week."

Friday morning it was Howard who greeted me, not Irene. "Penny called to say she must see Irene," he explained, "so I thought I'd stay home for the morning."

Good thought, Howard. Is this when I need the stun gun?

All hell broke loose when Penny barged in, slamming her briefcase on the table with a fierceness that made me jump. "Ina Faye Clark has accused Irene of stealing her recipe." She paused for effect, and then, "Cassoulet."

Silence for a long agonizing minute, and then Irene leapt to her feet. "I did no such thing. I took her recipe as a starting point and made some obvious improvements on it. That is not plagiarism!"

I was wracking my brain about cassoulet. It's a heavy, rich French stew usually with pork sausage, duck, lamb, always white beans. Definitely a winter dish, and if I remembered right, we had featured it in January—the so-called doldrums of winter. If this Clark person wanted to claim copycat, why had she waited until May?

Quietly, Howard asked, "What and how much does she want?"

I asked the basic question. "Who is Ina Faye Clark?"

Predictably, nobody answered my question. Penny brusquely said, "Damages. No amount yet. And she wants Irene to appear on her show and publicly apologize."

I gasped, Irene put her face in her hands, and Howard proved himself made of sterner stuff than I thought.

"No damages. She appears on Irene's show, so Irene can tell her how she adapted Ms. Clark's recipe to create her own dish." Without missing a beat, he turned to me and said, "Henny, please find out everything you can about this Ina Faye. And cassoulet. My memory tells me there isn't any one way to make that dish."

I felt like I was in a police drama—or a news story at the least—and being given my orders. Irene, by this time, was quietly sobbing but managed to wail, "I am ruined. I will never cook again." I thought that was a bit dramatic, but it wasn't my life being ruined. The phrase echoed in my mind—was this what Gabrielle had threatened? It was a far cry from murder, but it still was pretty awful.

"I don't feel well," Irene said, a hand to her forehead. I could have told us that a sinking spell was coming on her part.

Penny's response was no-nonsense. "Balderdash! We have work to do, a counter-campaign to plan."

Howard stood and gathered up Penny's briefcase, which so far she hadn't even opened. Handing it to her, he said, "My wife needs to rest. This has been a great shock. I'll be in touch." And with a gentle but persuasive hand on her elbow, he led her to the door. She was still sputtering as she went out.

I heard her ask in a staged whisper as she was forcibly marched to the door, "Did you report the threat on Irene's life to the authorities?"

Stunned, I whirled quickly to look at Irene, but she hadn't heard. She was still busy weeping into her hands. But I had clearly heard, and I was puzzled. Howard gave me to understand that he did not like Penny and did not trust her. I had thought I was the only one he told about the threat. But if he didn't tell her, how did Penny know?

Howard's answer did nothing to clear up the matter. It was a short and forceful, "No," and the next thing I heard was the door closing.

I was standing, ready to leave, when he returned.

He put a comradely arm around my shoulders, much different from his touch of Penny. "Henny, thank you for everything you do. Let me know what you find out. I'll report over the weekend on Irene. I'm sure she'll recover."

I nodded. There was nothing to say. I had my marching orders. At the door, as I turned to say goodbye to Howard, I heard Gabrielle's voice from the dining room.

"Now what the hell is wrong with you this time? Another of your convenient migraines?" Her tone was strident, and I could somehow picture her, arms akimbo, looming over her mother, who probably still huddled in her chair. *Chin up, Irene! Show a little of the haughty command now to your daughter.*

I carried that image with me on the long bus ride home.

There I was, not even noon on a Friday, and I was home for the day, nothing to do. Patrick was at the university. It was one of those times that I longed for a girlfriend, someone to whom I could say, "Let's splurge and go to The Promontory and have the lobster hash with a really good glass of white wine." I had a BLT at home with Topo Chico.

Ina Faye Clark was not exactly all over the internet. She did not have a web page, unless she used a pseudonym but what would be the point of doing that? Not popular enough for a Wikipedia page, but then neither was Irene. I'd thought about writing an entry for her but was somehow reluctant. I figured Irene had to earn fame on her own, though Penny seemed to think she could buy it.

I had to dig deep until I found Ina Faye's show—I felt we were on a first-name basis by then—on Saturday mornings on the Cooking Channel, not the same as the Food Network. Apparently, she'd won one of those cook-off things once and while it hadn't exactly catapulted her to fame, it had gotten her a shot at national TV.

In the next two hours, I watched four half-hour segments of Ina Faye's show and was convinced the only difference between Ina Faye and Irene was that Ina Faye had a national show, while Irene's only ran on a local channel. She would have her audience believe she was cooking from her home kitchen, which was supposed to look like a French country kitchen: dark wood cabinets, several of them glass fronted, and a beamed ceiling, a patterned tile floor and floral patterned ceramic tile on the backsplash, copper cookware hanging from overhead hooks. The walls were plaster, including an alcove where wineglasses of several shapes and sizes were arrayed. Below them, on the tile counter, sat a mind-boggling choice of wine and liquor.

Ina Faye seemed incapable of cooking anything without some form of alcohol in it. While I watched, she did a beef stew with prunes and red wine, a chicken pot with Riesling wine, an Alsatian dish with kraut and beer, and a poached chicken dish that used champagne instead of water or broth—showy but expensive. Ina Faye herself was not a natural showman. Someone had apparently told her to look at the camera, which she did so often that one wondered she didn't cut her hand off while chopping vegetables or spill the poaching liquid when she aimed for the sink. She was given to little trills of nervous laughter, and her voice was pitched too high to be pleasant. Irene could beat her hands down.

A search for "Ina Faye Clark cassoulet" came up empty—hmmm, a bit suspicious that. But I did find her Coquille St-Jacques, and it was pretty much spot-on for Irene's version. Let's hope Ina Faye doesn't find that one out.

Over the weekend I tried unsuccessfully to distract myself from worry about Irene with a mystery novel, some boring television, sushi with Patrick, and a long phone conversation with my mom during which I brightly assured that everything was wonderful, I expected a promotion any day (well, not a white lie if I became a bodyguard), no I hadn't met Mr. Wonderful yet. Yes, of course I'd love to have her come visit. I hadn't seen her since Christmas, and Mom had never been to Chicago. I'd love to show her the sights, but, no, now was not a good time.

I even searched the web for information on bodyguards. The Wikipedia entry was all about government officials and celebrities. Being a bodyguard or part of a bodyguard team to such people involved things I definitely wouldn't be doing—like searching cars for LED devices. They all carried guns, which I wasn't about to do, and they were mostly stern men in business suits and wraparound sunglasses. And they were on twenty-four-hour duty, never leaving their person alone. I would definitely be out of my league and noncompliant with a lot of the requirements.

How could I protect Irene if I didn't know what the risks were?

Somehow, I avoided talking to Patrick about most of this, answering in monosyllables and telling him instead about the plagiarism. As a scientist, he was shocked. As a man, he seemed to think it was a woman's problem, and I could solve it.

By Sunday night I was convinced either Irene or Howard would call to tell me not to show up at the studio Monday evening. Surely Irene was still indisposed. I jumped when the phone rang, but it was Gabrielle of all people.

She talked low, almost a whisper, as if she had her hand cupped around the phone and was making sure no one overheard the conversation. "We have to talk," she said.

I tried the line I'd used on my mother: now is not a good time. But she was persistent, and I finally agreed to meet her for a drink on Wednesday. Curiosity told me to suggest the next night, Monday, but a wiser part of me decided to let Gabrielle stew for a couple of days.

And I'd make her come to Hyde Park. I wasn't going to traipse up to the North Side for a drink. I know I was being petty, but I figured if she wanted to talk to me, she could come to me. She didn't seem to mind and said she'd Uber to whatever destination I chose. The Woodlawn Tap, a longtime neighborhood favorite on Fifty-Fifth Street, was a place where I felt comfortable going alone to wait for someone who might or might not show up. She probably wouldn't buy drinks either. For a moment, I wondered if I should take her to a pub, since she was not nearly of age to drink. Oh well, I wanted that Polish sausage sandwich, and I'd monitor what she had.

* * *

Having had no word from either Howard or Irene, I showed up on time Monday and found Irene already in the studio, toque in place, ready to work. The evening's shoot was a segment on three things to do with kale. It was a topic I'd strongly protested. I am of the school that believes if you add a little coconut oil to kale in the skillet, it makes it easier to throw out. But Irene was adamant. Kale, she said, is "in." So we did a kale sauté with beets and carrots, a kale Caesar salad (travesty!), and southern-style kale with a ham hock. Now there, to me, is an irony: if you're eating kale to be healthy, why would you combine it with a ham hock as though it were common everyday turnip greens? I'll take creamed spinach, thank you.

But the shoot went well. Irene seemed in a good mood, easy to work with, almost pleasant to be around. Neither of us mentioned Ina Faye Clark or Penny, so I was left with a lot of questions in my mind. But I thought the week was off to a good start.

Wednesday we actually scored a morning slot at the studio. We were scheduled to do a wonderful spring lamb stew. Even I knew that it was closely modeled on the classic Julia Childs recipe, but I sailed ahead and hoped Julia's heirs didn't see the show. After all, what were the odds? But then again, what were the odds that Ina

Faye would watch Irene? Which, of course, got me wondering again how she knew about the cassoulet.

Wednesday morning started badly. Irene's timing was off again, and I feared her effort to revive the outdated angel food cake recipe was doomed. Pointing out how lucky we were to have modern, high-speed mixers to whip egg whites, she insisted on giving a demonstration of how her grandmother used to beat the whites with a whisk. She put the whites on a ceramic platter, held it sideways in her lap, and beat away. Nothing happened for a while, and then Irene's hands got slippery, and she dropped the platter, which broke. A mess for me to clean up. We cancelled that portion of the show and, at the end of the morning, wrote angel food cake off as a bad idea. That put us one show behind, and I scrambled to think how we could make it up.

We were scheduled for a midafternoon shoot that day too, so I assumed we'd both just stay in the studio. Maybe eat some lamb stew. But she surprised me.

"Henrietta, I have an appointment in the Loop. I may be a little late getting back."

I looked up to see that Irene had shed the apron and donned a suit jacket. Instead of her purse, she carried a Coach briefcase designed for ladies. Hindsight doesn't do much good, but right there I should have thought of Howard and said, "I'm going with you." But I didn't know how to explain my presence, and I sensed that she was being private about this appointment. So all I said, was, "Don't worry about it. Go and have a good time." Inane, I know.

She tried to pass it off with a laugh that didn't work. "Oh, I doubt I'll have any fun."

Hungry, I helped myself to a good-sized bowl of the lamb stew, which meant there wouldn't be as much for the stage crew, but, hey, first come, first served. Marveling at how good the stew was, I busied myself with menus. As I reviewed our selections, something became crystal clear to me. We were going about everything—the show and the cookbook—in a scattershot way. We went willy-nilly from salads to entrees to desserts in a breathless three days. Viewers wouldn't know what to expect on any given day, so why should they tune in? We needed to do blocks of recipes—at least a week, maybe a month. My plan would be a hard sell to Irene, but I knew I was right.

I was so lost in making lists of topics and recipes that time got away from me, and suddenly it was two o'clock. *Irene should be back.* A frisson of fear came quickly and left with equal haste. No, of course, I wasn't worried. *But I should have gone with her.*

By three o'clock, I was—ah, concerned. By three thirty, with no word from Irene nor from Howard, I came close to panic. I called Howard's cell and got no answer. Calling Gabrielle was not an option. Calling Patrick might make me feel better but would do nothing for the situation. Besides, he was probably busy counting stars and asteroids or whatever.

What if she isn't back by the time the studio has scheduled the next shoot? What if . . . my cell phone vibrated, and I grabbed it with both hands. "This is Henny."

Chapter Six

"There's been an accident." Howard's voice was tense. "I'm in the emergency room with Irene. She's broken her left arm."

How bad am I that I said a silent prayer of gratitude that she was not left-handed? Then I asked the usual questions—where and how? I had a death grip on the phone because I could see my short-lived television career going down the tubes. I was worried for Irene . . . and selfishly for me.

"The ambulance brought her to Northwestern Memorial. I got here as soon as I could. They've given her something for pain and something to calm her down. X-rays show a clean break just above her wrist. Lots of swelling. They tell me they'll send her home in a splint-like device until the swelling goes down enough for a cast."

"What happened? How did she break it?" *And just what kind of an appointment results in a broken arm?* I was kicking myself for not going with her, but Howard's mind hadn't apparently gotten as far as bodyguards.

"An accident. She says clumsy. She was standing on a curb, waiting to cross Monroe Street, in the middle of a knot of people. When the light changed, and they all moved at once—you know how that happens—she fell off the curb. Says she thinks someone bumped into her by accident."

By accident? Hello, Howard! Aren't you the one who told me about a threat against her? What if someone pushed her? My mind was racing and my thinking not quite logical, but I knew a shove in a crowd would be hard to prove. "There must have been police. Did they question people?"

Howard seemed to be growing tired of my questions, and I couldn't blame him. But I could hear exasperation creeping into his voice. "A policeman came to the ER. He says two or three people stayed with her. Someone called the police, who called the ambulance. But nobody saw anything. She's lucky it wasn't her leg or hip."

The sixty-four-dollar question. "How long will she be out of commission?" For a brief moment there I wondered if I'd have to cook on screen—it would either hurtle me to stardom or sign my doom. I was uncertain.

"Doctor says it depends on her. How determined she is, how well she adapts to using only her right hand." He paused. "I'll call the network next and schedule at least a week, maybe two, of reruns."

Reruns! Why hadn't I thought of that? Two weeks would give me time to polish my new plan. "Ask for three," I suggested.

"Will you spend a few days choosing the programs? I've got all the tapes at the apartment. I can put them on a zip drive for you—say shows from three years ago. Don't want to do too recent."

"Of course, I'll do whatever I can to help. I can come pick up the zip drive."

"No. I want to keep Irene undisturbed. If she knew you were there, she'd want to tell you what to do about the show."

At least he knew his wife well. I doubted he was in for a pleasant time ahead. By contrast, my assignment sounded much better.

"I'll have a courier bring it to you first thing tomorrow morning."

It dawned on me that Howard really, really didn't want me at the apartment or near Irene. What was up with that? I decided to worry about it later and settle down for an evening in front of the TV. After all, I didn't have to get up and go to work early tomorrow morning.

I'd just settled down with a glass of wine and the remote in my hand, when my phone dinged at me. It was a calendar reminder. I was supposed to meet Gabrielle at the Woodlawn Tap in fifteen minutes. I'd make it if I hurried and if I drove. I was still in the slacks and oversize checkered shirt I'd worn to the studio that day, so I freshened my makeup, ran a brush through my hair—I really did look shaggy and needed a trim—and ran for my car.

The Woodlawn Tap is a neighborhood standby, known to regulars as Jimmy's in tribute to the former owner who has now passed on. Maybe a few tourists wander in, but the crowd is basically neighborhood folks and faculty and students from the university. Jimmy's is famous for cheap pitchers of beer, Polish sausage sandwiches, and fries that are world-class. The bar takes pride in its dark, pub-like atmosphere, with mismatched chairs, taped patches on the tears in some booth upholstery, and a bar top that had probably never been refinished. Elegant it is not, but it is comfortable and reassuring.

Patrick first brought me here, but I've been back lots by myself, especially when I crave a good hamburger. It's the kind of place where girls are not afraid to go alone—if someone who doesn't know better gives you any trouble, the staff is quick to jump in. It's also not the kind of place Gabrielle would ever choose. I'd like to say I chose it because I knew we could talk without interruption, but I think I also had a less noble motive. I had no idea what Gabrielle wanted to talk about, but I smelled trouble, and if I was right, I wanted to meet her on my turf, where I would be in charge. And she would be just a bit on edge, or so I hoped. As I would have been if she'd coerced me to meet her at Drink and Ink or Decibel Bar or some other Uptown watering hole. Did I forget to mention that I suggested to Patrick that he stop by after his evening lab? He would be a buffer for me, just as meeting at Jimmy's was a protective maneuver.

Gabrielle was sitting at the bar when I got there. I stood in the door for a moment looking at the picture she made with the big polished wood back bar behind her. Her hair seemed a lighter blonde than the last time I saw her, and she wore the same deliberately casual outfit—torn jeans and an outsized shirt, both of which shouted money. The effect was sort of a statement that Gabrielle was going slumming or something like that. She had apparently ordered a virgin Mary, and the man behind the bar, a substitute I didn't recognize, looked none too happy about it.

I blew off my tardiness with an airy "Sorry," picked up her drink, and headed for a booth. She followed like a well-trained dog.

"We might as well have supper," I said. "Burgers and hot dogs are great, but they're known for Polish sausage sandwiches."

Gabrielle wrinkled her nose. "I'll take a cheeseburger," she said. "Mayo, no mustard."

Out of sheer perverseness I had the Polish sausage with a beer.

Gabrielle looked around. "Is this an okay place? I mean, I won't get mugged when I leave, will I? You know, South Side and all . . . "

"Gabrielle," I said patiently, "this is Hyde Park. University of Chicago territory. You're safe unless you run down the middle of Fifty-Fifth Street stark naked at two in the morning."

She laughed a bit nervously.

"How's your mother?" I asked. "I don't like that story about her falling off a curb downtown."

She shrugged. "Irene isn't always as graceful and in command as she likes to be on the show. I'm sure she wasn't paying attention. She'll be all right, though right now she's behaving like a drama queen. Pain and all that." She was drawing circles with her finger in a bit of moisture on the tabletop.

Calling her parents by their first names was not lost on me. It was a not-so-subtle sign of disrespect, a flag of young-adult rebellion. I ignored it. "Howard didn't seem to think I should come see her. I think he wants her to forget about the show for a few days."

"Howard is overprotective," she scoffed. "Of everyone but me."

Here it comes—the poor little me spiel. I waited.

No one else would have noticed, but I did. Gabrielle took charge of the conversation. She looked directly at me and said, "I want you to find my father."

"Howard? He's at the apartment taking care of your mother." It was an instinctive answer, one that I hadn't thought through.

She looked scornful as she took another sip of her drink. "Howard is not my biological father. I thought you could have figured that out by now."

"Who is your father?" Dumb question number two.

Gabrielle was clearly losing patience. "I don't know. That's the whole point. I want you to find out."

I took a big sip of beer for strength. Why did this family seem to think I was their personal private eye? Howard expects me to protect Irene; now Gabrielle thinks I can find her biological father. "Gabrielle, I need more information." Maybe I should have just said, "No way, José. This is not my deal." But I didn't. I walked right into the trap.

For a moment, we were saved by the arrival of our food. I dug into my sandwich immediately, but Gabrielle eyed hers, examined it, taking the bun top off so she could inspect the ingredients, sniffing it as though the smell would tell her something besides that it would be delicious. At last she took one dainty bite. I, meanwhile, had taken a huge bite of my sausage and was savoring the spicy meat, wishing for sauerkraut on it.

"All I know," she said, "is that my *real* father has contacted my mother, and she's upset about it. But she won't talk to me about him at all. Neither will Howard."

I wanted to point out a few realities of life to this spoiled baby, like the fact that the only way I knew to find the answer to her question was to ask Irene. And since Irene obviously didn't want to talk about it, and since she's my boss, that wasn't on my agenda.

"Have you checked your birth certificate?"

She shook her head. "The state of Illinois will alter a birth certificate to show the adoptive parents instead of biological. Given the timing of when Irene was in France and when she married Howard, I assume my father is French. I presume he's from Paris, but he could be in the French boonies now for all I know."

Go find a Frenchman. She almost sounded like any Frenchman would do. Clearly, she had no clue about the difficulty of the task she was giving me. Wrong again. Her next words made it worse.

Gabrielle took a second small bite and nibbled on a lone French fry while she studied me. "I want you to get Irene to talk to you."

Easier said than done. "How do you know Howard is not your biological father?" At this rate, I was going to need another beer.

"I overheard them talking. They thought I was asleep, but I stood just inside the kitchen door and listened." It didn't seem to bother her at all that she'd eavesdropped on a private conversation.

It bothered me, though. I could see her in my mind's eye, poised just inside that swinging door, ear or eye to the crack. Still, I asked, "What else did you learn?"

She shrugged. "Just that whoever this man is, he's contacted Irene, wants to get to know me."

I had been raised not to eavesdrop, but I had also been raised by a loving mother. Sure, she frustrated me at times, but she was also the first person I turned to for advice and opinions. Obviously, Gabrielle did not enjoy that kind of relationship with Irene.

By nibbles, she was now halfway through her hamburger and had started on the fries—one at a time, of course. I squirmed in impatience.

"You can't just ask Irene?"

She gave me a pitying look. "You know better than that. You know how she is."

Frustrated at the way she dodged the question, I was forthright. "Why is it so important to you to know this man. What is he turns out to be poor"—I thought that was a great warning to her—"or a thief or something?"

Complacently, she smiled. "He won't be poor. He'll be handsome, and he'll have good manners." She stared off in space a minute, and then whipped her eyes back to mine. "Wouldn't it be exciting if he were a thief?"

"And if you never find out who or what he is?"

"I'll make Irene's life miserable." She paused thoughtfully. "Did you ever wonder how Ina Faye Clark knew about Irene and the cassoulet?" Calmly, she took another bite, while I did all I could to keep from leaping up, knocking the table into her lap, and screaming, "You bloody idiot!" Instead, I told her I needed to use the restroom—"All that beer," I joked—and excused myself. In the shabby restroom with its cracked mirror and dingy wallpaper, I took deep breaths and tried to control my indignation. Essentially, Gabrielle wanted me to spy on my boss, after she herself had betrayed her. Who knew what hellish revenge she'd take on me if I didn't help her? I wanted to cry out, "Lord, why me?" but I knew the answer to that one—I happened to be in the wrong place at the right time, or the right place . . . or however you wanted to look at it. It was sheer dumb bad luck.

When I got back to our booth, she was gone, the remains of her hamburger and most of the fries on the plate. She'd left something for me—a smiley face drawn on a cocktail napkin. It was Gabrielle's way of twisting the knife, smiling over the dilemma she'd given me.

I was still stewing, nursing my second beer, when Patrick found me. His lab, he explained, had run late. Too many students with too many questions.

"Hi, sunshine," he greeted me. "What put you in such a funk?"

"Gabrielle Foxglove," I muttered.

"Ah, yes. Where is she?" He looked around as though he expected her to crawl out from under the table any minute. "I was looking forward to meeting her. From what you said, I thought she would jump my bones."

I gave him what I hoped was a withering look and refrained from saying, "I didn't think girls interested you." Motioning to the hamburger remains, I said, "She disappeared while I was in the john taking deep breaths."

"Deep breaths in the john—must have been quite a scene. What happened?"

So I spilled the whole story about her desperation to find her biological father. He listened carefully and then tried to reason with me, which was the wrong thing at that moment. "I had a buddy in school who was adopted. He knew it all along, but he still was convinced that his life and his luck would change if he found his biological parents. It wouldn't, but there was no convincing him. I imagine Gabrielle feels that way too."

"She sabotaged her mother," I said, brushing aside his school buddy who may or may not have been a fiction. "She convinced Ina Faye Clark that Irene copied her cassoulet." There! I'd spit out the horrible part of it.

Patrick took a long slow sip of the beer he'd brought to the table. "Let's go back again to how Ina Faye Clark knew about the cassoulet."

"Gabrielle told her," I interrupted.

He held up a hand, palm outward, asking for patience, of which I had none. "Is Gabrielle smart enough for that? How would she have known about this Clark woman? How much does she know about cassoulet or any other dish? I bet not enough to be behind this particular bit of mischief."

If not Gabrielle, who? And why? And why did Gabrielle want to be responsible for something she didn't do? "She must have looked around on the internet for a likely TV chef. Why she chose cassoulet is beyond me. It was a dumb choice."

I'd forgotten the worst of the news and blurted out, "Irene fell off a curb on Monroe Street and broke her arm."

He set his beer down so hard it splashed on the table. "Whoa! Fell off? Who falls off a curb? Are they sure it was an accident? After what Howard told you, I'd be suspicious."

"You might," I said, "but it hasn't apparently occurred to Howard, and Gabrielle just blindly attributed it to Irene being clumsy."

"Is she?"

"Clumsy? No more than anyone else."

"You need that personal alarm. Where is it?"

I held up my keys, with the alarm dangling. "Irene needed it. Not me."

"We're back to that question: who would want to hurt her? You suppose it's the biological father?"

We could sit there all night and never solve that, and now I was tired. Exhausted emotionally and the beer was making me sleepy. "Finish your beer, so I can go home," I said.

He did, and we walked home in companionable if not happy silence. That night as I lay half asleep, I blamed not Gabrielle but Patrick for planting a new worry in my mind. Perhaps Irene really was in danger—from the man who fathered her daughter. And then, suddenly, I remembered I had one clue to Gabrielle's father—that photograph I'd found. But it was a slim clue. I drifted off, dreaming of strange blond men, all courting Irene.

It was the next morning before I remembered I had driven to Jimmy's. Then I had to walk back to get my car.

Chapter Seven

Irene would miss at least two weeks of the show, two weeks that I guiltily anticipated with happiness because I expected less pressure, less drama, life at a slower pace. It didn't turn out that way at all.

Penny was on me daily about the cookbook. I placated her with outlines, a general introduction, sample recipes, but nothing would satisfy her until she had a complete manuscript, which obviously wasn't going to happen soon. I suggested she consult a book designer about cover art and layout. But I couldn't ignore her strident voice on the phone, and I found myself compiling recipes late into the night. I kept remembering a cookbook my grandmother had—The *Southern Living Party Cookbook.* I wished for it now. It had things like scrambled eggs you could do hours before a brunch and save. Or crepes.

We couldn't, of course, finalize anything without Irene's approval, but Penny brushed that little detail aside. She chose the title *Irene's Favorite Forty*, and she liked my idea of menus. So I needed at least forty menus. By the end of the two weeks, I had six and an impatient publicist.

Then there was the show. I had to remind Penny constantly that the show took priority over the cookbook. The latter would exist only to boost the former. She wanted to rename the show *Irene's Favorite Forty*, but I saw the danger in that—limiting ourselves to forty recipes. I did commit to developing more menu shows, fewer that were single-dish oriented.

"You can't base a half hour on avocado toast," she declared. "What do you serve with it?"

"Wine," I shot back. But she had a point.

We got by on reruns for three weeks—after all, that was only three shows. One show was on shepherd's pie, a dish that trendy authorities declared no one in the twenty-first century should still eat. I drew the line at congealed salads but there was a tape of composed salads—Cobb and the classic Salad Niçoise—that I used. And then, Sloppy Joe, figuring I was pitching the show to an audience of cooks, not chefs, who would happily feed their kids Sloppy Joe. Irene had done a show on wine casserole, but it dawned on me that it would make great Sloppy Joes. So I did an intro suggesting that change, and the rerun got better ratings than almost any of Irene's live broadcasts.

In general, the reruns got a good reaction. I studied them to see what made them work and realized it was Irene. At her best, she was relaxed and had a certain charm about her, sophisticated but not too much. Could she recapture that? Could I help her, even while saving her life? Struck me as a tall order.

I taped a little introduction, which gave me my first talking role on camera. Looking straight at the imagined audience, I explained that Irene had suffered a minor accident but would return soon. Meantime, she had picked these favorite older shows just for you. It was a little white lie, but I thought it worked well.

The network warned Howard that it would only tolerate reruns for so long, but I put that little worry out of my mind for the time being.

Ina Faye Clark reared her head and demanded her showtime on the first day I was alone in the studio. My encounter with her was so unexpected that it caught me off guard. She walked into the studio just as a show finished. I was doing my live two minutes, teasing people with the next show and hoping they would be intrigued by composed salads. Midsentence I was distracted by this tiny woman who came in despite the flashing "On Air" sign and stood quietly, clutching her purse as though someone would steal it. It was an outrageously unfashionable leatherette bag with fake tooling.

The minute the cameraman called it a wrap, I made a beeline for this intruder. "Did you have business in here?" I was blunt because I was angry that she had almost interrupted the show.

She smiled and held out a hand. "I'm Ina Faye Clark, and I'm ready to tape that guest spot."

She was much smaller than she looked on camera, and I decided that she must stand on a stool, and the cameraman knew how to shoot to, uh, enlarge her presence. But at that moment, I felt like a giant towering over her with every inch of my five-foot-four.

I sputtered. "You're in New York." It wasn't meant as a question.

"No, I'm right here. Staying at the Hampton Inn downtown." She handed me a hotel business card, with a phone extension scribbled on it.

Then she said, "I want to shoot the show, making cassoulet." Her tone was sweet but firm, and she never let go of her death grip on her purse.

"Let's sit down," I said and led the way to the two stools on the set. The crew who were wrapping up could just work around us. "Cassoulet is a winter dish. It's May."

That smile again. "I know, but it's important to set the record straight about that dish." Reluctantly, she set her purse on the counter.

"How can you miss taping your own show? I mean, do you do a lot ahead? Irene doesn't like to do that. She says they should be fresh . . . and seasonal." A voice inside me said *stop blathering.*

She squirmed a bit, but she never lost that too-sweet smile. "My show has been cancelled. That's really why I'm here. I want to take over Irene's show."

Take over? "Oh, you misunderstand. She's not left the show permanently. It was just a small accident. Broken arm. She'll be back in a week or so, even if she's one-armed." Pretty clever.

"I'll tape tomorrow and tell her audience the truth about what's going on."

Howard! Where are you when I need you? "You still misunderstand. Irene's husband produces the show. He's not about to replace his wife with you."

Tracing the ridiculous embossed design on that purse with her finger, she replied without looking at me. "I've spoken with the network and with Ms. Aldrich. I think we can work things out."

I've met some sly and nasty people in my life, but Ina Faye took the cake. She even beat Gabrielle. I wasn't sure if she was sincere about taking over the show or if she was edging toward blackmail. I wasn't about to let her get away with either, but at that moment I really wished I'd never heard of cassoulet. Shoot, I wished I didn't know a thing about cooking.

"Since you tried to sabotage Irene with the network and Penny Aldrich, don't you think it's time you talked to Howard Foxglove?" I thought it was a pretty good answer, but it didn't ruffle her.

"Of course. You'll give me his number, and I'll call him as soon as I leave here."

I reached under the counter for the pad of sticky notes I knew was there—and it wasn't. I had to scramble ungracefully over cables and around cameras, run to the office to grab my purse, and make my way back to the kitchen set, while Miss Cool Ina Faye watched. I swear I saw her smile a bit, but it wasn't a friendly smile.

I scribbled Howard's cell number on a sticky note, tore it off, and handed it to her with an ungracious, "There you are."

"Good." She finally opened that blasted purse, slipped the note in, and pulled out a larger piece of paper. "Here's a list of ingredients I'll need tomorrow. You can get them. I'll just run along now."

Before I could protest or even explain that we didn't have a taping slot scheduled tomorrow or any day soon, she was gone. I willed her to trip over a cable, but it didn't happen. When I looked at the list, my mood grew even darker. For one thing, it was long, with such things as lamb shoulder. I for one was not going to bone a lamb shoulder. Way too much work and too much chance to hurt myself badly with a knife.

It took me a minute, but I realized that Ina Faye had outfoxed herself. This list was nothing like the ingredients in Irene's cassoulet. For one thing, Irene felt as I did about lamb shoulder. We'd used boneless stew meat. And ketchup in cassoulet? Never.

With trembling hands, I punched in Howard's cell phone number and made a note to put him on speed dial. I had to talk to him before Ina Faye got to him.

Howard listened as I poured out the story and simply said, "I'll handle it. Don't bother with that list of groceries—except prepare a list of what Irene actually used, so we'll have some record."

That evening Patrick found me at my dining table, poring over notes. "What are you doing this late at night?"

When I told him about Ina Faye, his first reaction was disbelief. "You're kidding! She must have a heck of a lot of nerve. Scientists do occasionally steal from each other, but they never own up to it, and they're ostracized when it's revealed."

"Everybody plagiarizes," I said with a sigh. But I wasn't really discouraged. The two versions of cassoulet were proving to be quite different from each other. Why hadn't Penny checked before she gave any time or space to this imposter? A failing imposter at that. She'd lost her own show, probably for plagiarism.

Then it struck me. What a hoot if it was really the other way around, and Ina Faye had stolen from Irene? I bet I could prove it with research, like matching calendars to see if Ina Faye's cassoulet show came after Irene's. But it wouldn't be worth it. As long as Ina Faye was no threat to Irene, I'd simply let it bubble along.

Howard called the next morning. "Ina Faye has checked out of the Hampton Inn and supposedly left Chicago." He paused. "I don't think we've heard the last of her but at least for now she's not a problem."

There was such a long silence on the other end that I finally asked, "Howard? Are you still there?"

He cleared his throat and said yes, he was still there, just distracted for a minute. "Irene wants to see you. Can you come today?"

"Of course. I'll come in the afternoon. I've already almost missed the morning bus." That was an exaggeration, but I'd have to really hustle to make that bus, and my mind was still set on Ina Faye and cassoulet. When I went north, I wanted to have the evidence in hand.

"I've watched the show, Henny. The taped opening is good, and I like the live close. Irene hasn't asked about the show at all, and I haven't suggested she watch, though I have a tape of it. I'm not sure why she asked to see you. Makes me a bit nervous, frankly." He tried to smooth that over with a chuckle that came out sounding strangled.

I found myself reassuring him. "I'll come as soon as I can, Howard. It will be all right."

I wasn't quite as convinced as Howard that Ina Faye had gone, although a call to the Hampton Inn confirmed that she had checked out. Still, I was on alert, half expecting her to knock on my door any minute. If she found me at the studio, she could surely find my apartment. Finally, toward noon, I decided with relief that she really was gone, at least for a while. But any relief I felt about Ina Faye's disappearance was countered by worry over Irene. If she was ignoring the show, why did she want to see me?

I checked the bus schedule and headed north.

It had only been—what? a week?—since I'd seen Irene, but she was a changed person. It wasn't just the cast on her left arm. It was the whole air about her. She reminded me of a deflated balloon. The imperious chef had been replaced by an insecure woman who somehow seemed to have shrunk. If I didn't know Irene, I would have said she was scared—and maybe she was.

She sat in one of those big chairs in the sunroom and at first was unaware that I had come in, so I stood a minute in the doorway and studied her. When I moved to greet her, she held out her arms as though to hug me, something the Irene I knew had never ever done. But her movement with her left arm was awkward, and I wondered if the cast was heavy. I wondered too if stress had brought the tremor back, but it would be hard to tell with that cast.

When she spoke, her voice was low, her words a bit slurred—or was that my imagination? "Henrietta, it's sweet of you to come see me. Tell me about the show. Who's doing the cooking?"

Surely Howard had told her we were in reruns. I looked at him, and he shook his head ever so slightly. I had no idea what he meant by that, so I plunged ahead. "You are, Irene. Just a few years ago. We're rerunning your most popular shows. Ratings are pretty good so far, at least for the first few shows."

She looked puzzled. "I must get back. My viewers need new recipes. Henrietta, I want you to start finding things for me to cook. I just . . . I don't know when I'll be back." She looked wistfully at the cast on her arm, as though wishing it away, and then at Howard, who nodded enigmatically again.

"You'll have to regain your strength," he said, nicely dodging her unspoken question.

"Howard, do be a dear and get us a pitcher of iced tea and some cakes or something. And give me a moment to talk to Henrietta. We have girl and cooking talk to do."

"Of course, my dear," he said and then he was gone. But while he went toward the kitchen, I heard a loud noise from the bedroom area of that cavernous apartment. It sounded as though someone had dropped something heavy. And then I thought I heard a muffled oath. Irene either didn't hear anything or chose to act like she didn't.

When I asked about the noise, she said too quickly, "A workman is installing a window air conditioner unit. The bedrooms get so hot in our muggy summers."

I knew she was lying.

With Howard out of the room, she quickly seemed to regain her vigor. She sat up straight and turned to me. "Henrietta, I don't know anyone I can trust but you. I can't think clearly at all. I think it's the medicines I'm taking. You must help me. And you must take over the show. I'm afraid to come back. I haven't told Howard, but I didn't trip off that curb. Someone shoved me—hard."

Chapter Eight

Irene barely whispered those last words before Howard was back with a tray holding glasses and ice, a pitcher of tea, and what looked to be a plate of sliced banana bread. Irene shrank into her chair.

My head was spinning. Was she trying to tell me Howard was the villain in all this? To make conversation, I inquired after Gabrielle.

Before he could answer me, Irene echoed the question in a plaintive voice. "Where is she, Howard? I haven't seen her in days. Is she hiding from me?"

"Irene, you remember. She's visiting friends in Winnetka for a few days."

So Howard was alone with Irene, and she thought she was being drugged. Things got more and more strange. Although it was not true, I said, "I'd have thought she'd stay and help you care for Irene."

Rather distantly, Howard said, "I have a home health care person who comes in during the day. She's straightening Irene's room right now."

My mind reeled. They had different stories about the noise in the back, and I began to suspect it was neither a workman nor a home health care person. But who and what was it? And did Howard let slip that they didn't share a bedroom? Not very European of them. And Gabrielle—my imagination kicked in, and I saw her in my mind's eye locked in a bathroom, kicking the door. *Calm down, Henny.*

An unexpected surge of panic rose in my throat, and I had to get out of there. It felt like I bolted, but in truth I exited politely. Irene clutched my hand a bit too tightly, and Howard put a so-called affectionate hand on my shoulder, while guiding me to the door.

"I don't know how to help her," he whispered. "She's lost her spark. I'm so glad we have you to help us, dear Henny."

And I was out the door before I could snap, "Stop overmedicating her."

I sat at my dining table staring at a legal pad with a list of names on it, but I could make no sense of them: Penny, Gabrielle, Ina Faye Clark, the mysterious stranger. Reluctantly, at the bottom I added Howard's name. Why would any or all of these people want to hurt Irene? Until today I'd believed Patrick's sort of romantic theory that it was Gabrielle's biological father who was frightening Irene. I had smugly figured out that he was threatening Irene because she would not allow him access to their daughter, but now I'd found two flaws in that theory: she herself told me someone pushed her off that curb, but she didn't say who, and I could only guess that she felt the shove but didn't see the perpetrator or that it was someone she didn't recognize. Would this mysterious man, once her lover, be so dastardly as to hire someone to do his dirty work? I wrote dastardly on the margin of my page and circled it, just because it was such a great word that had popped unbidden into my mind.

The romantic part of all this, of course, was the affair that had created Gabrielle, and I was just nosy enough—and affection-starved myself—that I wanted details. But I could hardly come right out and ask Irene.

Something that didn't fit at all: the noise I'd heard in the back of the apartment. If Gabrielle was really off visiting friends, who was back there? The visiting nurse? If so, why hadn't Irene said that? Was the nurse male? I really thought I'd heard a male voice, even though it was quickly stifled.

Howard was an even bigger problem for me. I'd thought he was, after all these years, still head over heels about Irene. And yet today he had acted so weird, like he was keeping a secret. Although he had called me to visit Irene, once I got there, he didn't confide in me as he had previously but instead seemed relieved when I was anxious to rush out the door.

Irene's plea for help stirred the pot of my confusion. Sometimes as we worked on the show, I used to think she was a better actress than a chef, and she sure was playing a role now—that of a pitiful patient, overmedicated and slightly confused. But how could I help her, short of kidnapping her to keep her away from the medications? And how could I ever get her back to the charming yet commanding presence needed for the show? I'd counted on Howard to do all that, and now I was suspicious of him, almost afraid of him for Irene.

None of it made sense, and the longer I stared at that piece of paper, the worse things seemed to get. Patrick's special knock on the door—he had a code to tell me it was him—jarred me out of my funk.

But when I opened the door, it was not Patrick's face I saw. I found myself looking at a mirror image of myself, albeit taller and better dressed—but the long blonde hair. Okay, her hair, loose to her shoulders, framed a prettier face than mine, but I knew we were cut from the same college-sorority-days cloth. As I blinked, Patrick said, "Look who's here!"

I almost shouted, "Who?" but I was momentarily dumbstruck. What was Patrick doing with a beautiful and sort of sexy blonde? And why was my first instinct to grab him and proclaim, "He's mine." *Control yourself, Henny. He is not yours. He is your best friend forever, and he's gay. This must be some mistake.*

"Henny, meet my cousin, Madison. She's interviewing for a graduate fellowship at the university tomorrow, and she's spending the night, so she'll be sure to be on time tomorrow."

Brushing her hair back off her face, Madison added, "Call me Maddie."

I was reminded of that wonderful line from the poetry of Gwendolyn Brooks, "White girls be always playin' with their hair." I forced myself to say, "Hi, Maddie. Come on in."

"I'm going to take Maddie to supper and thought maybe you'd come with us. She wants a good old-fashioned cheeseburger, so I guess we'll go to Jimmy's. Want to come?" He looked like an eager puppy, and I got the sense he wanted me to approve of this cousin of his. Was she really his cousin?

Stop it! The day for you to be jealous is when he brings a drop-dead gorgeous male hunk for you to meet. "Come on in and let me run a comb through my hair and grab my purse."

They came in, and Maddie ingratiated herself with me by exclaiming over my bay window with its window seat. "I'd sit here and read all day. Too bad your apartment doesn't have these windows, Paddy."

Paddy? Yep, they're cousins. Only a cousin would use a nickname like that. Not that Henny gave me any room to talk.

We had a jolly dinner, and I kept my troubles to myself, except to say that the show was doing okay with reruns and I hoped Irene would be back in a week or so. Patrick gave me a long look. He knew I was covering up something, but we would talk about that later.

Maddie was applying for a teaching fellowship in environmental and urban studies at the university. She had an English degree from Northwestern and had done a year's clerkship or whatever in Oxford at St. Hilda's College, but she didn't want to be that far from home long enough to earn a graduate degree. I was a bit intimidated, because what she was studying and the field she'd be doing research in sounded like a world-changing or world-saving one, whereas I wasn't sure I was doing much for the world by serving as Irene's gofer.

* * *

Two days later, Howard called. "Irene is feeling some better, and she'd like you to come up for the day tomorrow to talk about recipes and menus."

Sigh. Another trip on public transportation, carrying my notebooks. I contemplated driving, but the Outer Drive still intimidated me. Reluctantly, I agreed to come, then scolded myself for being unsympathetic. "I'm glad she's better, Howard. How are you holding up?"

"Me?" He seemed surprised that I would ask. A nervous chuckle was followed by, "I'm holding up all right. Irene's got a bit of her old spark back."

I took that to mean she was less subservient, more demanding. And the next day I found out I was right. Irene opened the door herself and greeted me with a brisk, "Good morning, Henrietta. I think it's about time we got some work done."

And just what does she think I have been doing all week? No polite greetings, no update on her arm, not even an inquiry about the reruns. She simply led the way to the dining room, and I followed like her obedient puppy dog, which I guess wasn't so far off as an analogy. To my relief, a tray on the table held the coffeepot and two cups. Where, I wondered, is Howard?

In silence, I opened the carryall that I used as a briefcase and put a legal pad on the table, pulled a couple of pens from my purse, and sat down, ready for business.

Irene glanced over her shoulder, looking almost wary, and then in a hurried gesture used her right hand to reach into her pocket and draw out a small baggie with pills in it and what appeared to be a note. She pointed to my purse, and nodded approval when I slipped the baggie into the bag without looking at it. Then, with a slight sigh of satisfaction, she said, "Howard tells me you've planned some menus. Let's see."

I fished some notes out of the carryall and laid them on the table, but all the while that strange packet seemed to burn a hole in my purse. I itched to read that note.

Irene meanwhile was studying my notes. "These are old-fashioned dishes. Common everyday American food. Where's my signature French touch?" She wasn't exactly angry about it, but she clearly wasn't happy.

My one-word answer startled her. "Gone," I said flatly.

"Gone?" she echoed.

"Irene, French has been done and done well by, forgive me, better-known chefs, people like Jacques Pépin and Julia Child, even Craig Claiborne. Middle Eastern foods are trendy today—tahini and shakshuka, baba ghanoush, dolma, falafel—all things you don't cook and don't eat. But you do some American cooking, without recognizing it."

I took a deep breath and hurried on before she could interrupt me. "Since the mid-1980s, when James Beard died, American food has been ignored. It gets more and more unfashionable every day."

"Because it's boring." The lofty, superior tone crept back into her voice.

"But that's what you can change," I said. "You can become the chef who reinvented American cuisine, made it popular again, just as Beard once did. Sure, some of it needs updating. But I've been doing some internet research on this, and it's a big thing now to say millennials don't eat meatloaf, they don't eat Sloppy Joe, or even chicken pot pie. But that's not true. We reran the program you did on Sloppy Joe—actually, you called it wine casserole—and it got a great reaction, even a mention in the *Sun-Times* cooking column. I saved the clipping for you." I pulled out my strongest piece of evidence, a rumpled newspaper clipping, and pushed it toward her.

"Sloppy Joe?" Disdain dripped from the words. "It comes in a can. That Hunt's company, I believe. I never fixed that."

"You did, you just didn't realize it. I did a short intro, telling viewers they could use your wine casserole for sandwiches, and it would be an upscale, delicious Sloppy Joe. It's true. I tried it myself, and it's great. My friend Patrick liked it a lot too."

"But to compete with a canned product." She shuddered at the thought.

"That's just it," I said. "They don't make that anymore. Your audience doesn't cook out of a can. You have to show them how to make Sloppy Joe from scratch. Even adding that little red wine."

She looked skeptical but she was listening, and I prattled on, getting so carried away that I was mentioning things like a slot as visiting chef at the James Beard House. Now that perked her up right away.

"Do you have recipes?"

"Don't you want to develop your own?" I asked.

"Oh, *mais oui.*" Then she caught herself. "But of course. I simply need a starting point. I will get Howard to help me in the kitchen right away."

I pushed three recipes at her—chicken pot pie, shepherd's pie, and meatloaf. They had come straight off the internet, except for the meatloaf that was my mom's recipe. "See what you can do with these. And look up James Beard on the net." Would Howard have to do it all or would Irene try to master one-handed cooking? The cast would be a problem.

"He published a few cookbooks, didn't he?"

That was her way of dismissing Beard, slighting all his many other accomplishments for cooks and restaurants and the American eating public. But I had hooked her.

I left the apartment without ever seeing Howard, which was both a relief and a puzzle. Why wasn't he hovering?

On the long bus ride home, I could barely resist pulling out that packet of pills to read the note. I did reach in a couple of times to make sure it was still floating around in the bottom of the purse. I just knew if I pulled it out an undercover cop would bust me for illegal possession, though of what I wasn't sure.

Home at last, I bolted my door as though demons were following me and threw my bag on the table, pulling those contraband pills out. The note, in Irene's bold handwriting, commanded, "Have these pills analyzed. Tell no one."

Just how she thought I could follow both those directives was beyond me. I had no idea how to go about having a handful of little white pills tested. For starters, though, I didn't think it was smart to handle them. Did fingerprints adhere to pills? I counted them by pushing them aside through the baggie—eleven pills, with numbers and letters on them that meant nothing to me.

Patrick! Where was Patrick when I needed him?

Chapter Nine

Patrick was where he often was, too often for my taste, but then I had to remind myself I had no claim on his time. He was at the university, studying the stars. Finally, after an hour of staring at the pills on the table and worrying about Irene, I dialed his cell phone.

"What's up, Henny?" I swear if they were eavesdropping, his colleagues must have thought I was male, maybe even a romantic interest of his.

I tried to be casual. "Are you coming home soon?" Casual, as in having a death grip on my phone.

"Is it an emergency?" He sounded concerned, and I mentally kicked myself. No, of course it wasn't an emergency. I just had eleven white pills I didn't know what to do with. I couldn't tell him that over the phone.

"Oh, of course not. I just . . . well, when you come home . . . I need some help."

"Are you lying on the floor with a broken leg?"

Darn him! Why could he always make me laugh? "Of course I'm not. I just got home from Irene's, and I need some advice. That's all."

"Okay. I'll be along shortly."

Shortly turned out to be two hours, during which I recounted the pills, tried to search online for a picture that looked like them, dabbled in Facebook, and found that James Beard was not nearly as interesting as he had been yesterday.

When Patrick finally knocked on my door, I had to unbolt the door at his knock—forgot that my paranoia had led me to throw the dead bolt. And there he was in a crisp plaid shirt and fresh jeans.

"Why the secrecy, Henny?"

"You'll see," I whispered conspiratorially as I led him to the table.

"What you got?" He stared at the pills.

"Pills." Obvious answer but by this time I was all about drama. "Irene's pills. I don't know what they are."

He stared at me as though I was missing the obvious. "Ask her."

"No, you don't understand." Shifting nervously from one foot to the other, I explained how Irene had smuggled them to me with that commanding note.

"Okay. Take them to a pharmacist and ask him or her what they are. They have those handy reference books with pictures and everything."

I sighed. Patrick did not get it at all. "A pharmacist will want to know where I got them, and they might be illegal or something like that."

Patrick sank into one of the chairs at the table, his whole body expressing weary frustration. "Henny, you're making a big deal out of this. When it really isn't. But I'll tell you what. I'll take them to the pharmacology department—if I can find it—and ask someone, a graduate student, what they are."

"You mustn't tell anyone where they came from," I whispered and then wondered why I was whispering.

"Cross my heart," he said solemnly and made the full gesture. But his eyes were laughing, and I knew he was laughing at me as he left.

Patrick wasn't laughing when he came back the next evening.

* * *

OxyContin.

Shocked and speechless, I sat there for a long moment before my brain kicked back in. I knew, as did most people, how dangerous that opioid was—not just addiction, though that loomed large, but complications. Most doctors weaned patients off it as quickly as they could, yet Irene's broken arm was two weeks into healing now. Seemed to me a reputable physician would have given her something less powerful—like aspirin.

Instinct told me to rush to the phone and tell her not to take any more pills. But of course I couldn't do that. And when I stopped to think I realized she wasn't taking them. She was squirreling them away. But then why did she act like she was medicated? Clearly, out of sight and hearing of Howard, she was quite lucid.

Patrick sat watching me process all this without saying a word. Not until I jumped up and began pacing did he speak.

"Sit down."

"Can't. I'm too upset. I don't know what to do."

"Walking won't help. What are your options?"

"Why did Howard ask me to protect her, when he's trying to kill her?"

That brought Patrick to his feet. "Whoa! Cut the dramatics." He took my shoulders, gently but still, and pushed me back down on the couch. Then he sat next to me. "Answering a question with a question doesn't help either."

I sort of sobered. "I can confront Howard. Not a good option. He'll deny everything." I thought for a minute. "I can call her doctor."

He did the worst thing. He laughed. Out loud. "You can't invade the privacy between a physician and his patient. Even I know that."

"She's already stopped taking the pills, so I don't have to worry about that."

"Unless whoever gives them to her catches on."

I shifted to look at him in dismay. He'd come up with a whole new terror I hadn't thought of. But right at that moment, Irene went out of my mind, and Patrick took it over. He was wearing one of those blue shirts that accented his eyes, and in spite of my deadly earnest attitude, his eyes were smiling at me. I wanted to throw myself at him, have him hold me and comfort me. Instead, I jumped off the couch before temptation could lead me into a ludicrous situation.

Completely changing the subject I blurted out, "Have you had supper? I'm going to make hamburger Stroganoff."

He grunted. "Hamburger? Want me to go get some tenderloin?"

I shook my head. "No, this is for the blasted cookbook. We're trying—okay, I'm trying—to come up with recipes working parents can use to feed their families. And most of them can afford a lot more hamburger than tenderloin. Irene will go for it because she thinks it's a classy dish, and Stroganoff may not be French, but it's foreign enough to be exotic in her mind."

He snorted. "I'm in. I'll go get a bottle of wine and come back to do a salad."

He left, and I had no idea what to do next. Except cook, which usually calms me. I got out my cast-iron skillet and put a pot of water on to boil for the pasta. I wiped the mushrooms with a damp paper towel and sliced them, stems and all, diced a bit of onion, and lost myself in the recipe. I was just adding beef broth and tomato paste to the skillet, when Patrick walked in with a salad already made. I turned up the flame under the pasta water, and within fifteen minutes, we were silently eating, both of us enjoying the meal . . . and the silence.

Patrick broke it, pushing his empty plate away and asking, "So what's next? What do you really know about Howard Foxglove?"

"Not much," I admitted, scraping up the last bits of my dinner. "He's a puzzle. I think he loves Irene, and I think he's doing his best to protect her, but maybe his judgment is skewed?" How did that come out a question? Because I wasn't sure if I really believed that. I took a deep breath. "He seems to have money, pays all the bills for Irene to be a TV star, and yet he worries about money, from the price of a steak at Morton's to the cost of producing a cookbook."

"Looks like you've got tomorrow's work cut out for you."

Of course! Howard had told me to work from home for a few more days, choosing recipes for when we began to film. I already had the Stroganoff, and there was another week of reruns in the can. I had tomorrow free, and Howard might actually be easier to research online than Irene. And maybe I'd find out something about Gabrielle's father at the same time. "I'll start tonight," I said, suddenly clearing the table by stacking all the dishes in my old waitress-style one-arm carry.

"I'm outta here. Thanks for dinner. I'll check with you tomorrow. I'm gonna meet Maddie for a drink."

I ran a sink of hot, soapy water, practically threw the dishes into it, and put the skillet to soak—something you should never do to an iron skillet, and I knew better. But before you could blink, I was booting up my computer. And not even one whit jealous that he was meeting Madison. Wait! Maybe I was, just a bit jealous.

Ancestry.com seemed like a logical starting place to me, and I accepted their free get-acquainted month. But that was limited to the United States, and if my suspicions were true, I would have to cross the pond in my search. I didn't yet want to pay for that. Every time I typed "Foxglove" into Google, I got a hundred hits about the plant and warnings about its toxicity. Finally, I typed in "Foxglove family." Still brought botanical references but also a cluster of Foxglove families near an Illinois town named Kankakee. Sounded like a native American tribe to me.

I searched for obituaries, figuring they would list survivors, and finally I found Howard! Second son of an English duke, my foot! He was a good, old farm boy from Illinois. His father, Russell Foxglove, died in 2012. If I figured Howard was fifty, he should have graduated from high school in 1987. I pulled up Kankakee High School. Nothing. I went to a map of Kankakee County and methodically began searching high school records in nearby small towns.

On the sixth try, I found him at Watseka High School, a school with fewer than four hundred students. Who knows what it was in the eighties? There was Howard, looking remarkably like he does today—no chin, fair hair, skin so pale that he almost looked invisible. And young. It was the Howard of today, only younger—and more unremarkable. It was also, to my surprise, the man in the photo I'd found. So there went a clue to Gabrielle's parentage.

Surprise! Someone in Watseka, or Pittwood, where the school was located today, had the foresight to digitalize old yearbooks. The 1987 book had a paragraph about each student—it said Howard was shy and quiet, had few friends, and would be attending Kankakee

Community College. His favorite subject was French, and his favorite teacher, Miss Althea Goodman, who taught French. No surprise there. That meant Howard had missed a lot of the social experience of college. He'd almost certainly lived at home and been a day student.

Why did an Illinois farm boy study French with apparent intensity? I looked at a few other graduate entries, and no one else mentioned their favorite teacher. On an impulse, I searched for Althea Goodman Watseka—nothing. So I dug into the obituary files in the Kankakee newspaper, and there she was—died ten years after he graduated, which meant she was alive when he went to the community college.

Her obituary was unremarkable. She fit the stereotype of so many teachers. Back in the day, long before Howard hit school, they were called spinsters, women for whom teaching was their whole life. That was about all except for a gem at the bottom: before her death, she endowed a scholarship fund for one worthy student from Watseka High, to be granted every ten years. The first such scholarship, in 1991, went to Howard Foxglove. I wondered just how close that relationship was.

Stifling a yawn, I realized it was past midnight. I didn't have to report to work tomorrow, but still, if I wanted to get much done, I'd best go to bed.

Howard strolled through my dreams wearing a Cheshire cat grin that clearly said, "I have a secret." Between tossing and turning, I wondered how someone with that background amassed enough money to rent a North Shore apartment (well, it was almost on the shore) and fund a TV show. It was four before I slept, and I never did sleep soundly.

Chapter Ten

Next morning as I lingered in bed, feeling almost like I had a hangover, I heard Patrick's distinctive knock on the door and heard his key turn in the lock. I jumped out of bed, still in the jeans and T-shirt I'd worn last night, my hair going ten ways, and my teeth unbrushed—oh well, I just wouldn't get close to him. That's part of the beauty of our relationship. No pretense, take each other as we are, but don't get too close. I batted aside the part of me that thought closeness would be great.

"That's it, Henny. Get up and get after the day!" He was laughing at me.

"I worked late last night."

"I partied late. Maddie is a hoot. Much more fun than when we were kids . . . "

Thanks for telling me I missed a fun evening. I was all set for pout, when he jolted me out of it. "Maddie's going to come by around noon to take you to lunch. I told her you'd be here all day and would probably welcome a break."

I could feel myself getting stubborn. How did he know if I'd welcome a break or not? What made him think he could speak for me? Poor Maddie—I was really starting to dislike her, and she'd done nothing to earn it. I poured water into the coffeemaker so vigorously that it splashed all over, dousing Patrick, who yelped.

"I guess I'll be going. Have a great day, Henny." And he was gone.

Settled at the computer with my coffee, I got lost in my search for the truth about Howard Foxglove. By midmorning, with the help of a phone call to the registrar's at Kankakee Community College, in which I pretended to be a representative of a headhunter agency, I knew that Howard had earned a B.A. in general studies at the college in 1994. Somewhere along the way he lost a year.

"A note says he went on to the Wharton School of Business," the assistant added helpfully. Made me feel a bit guilty because I'd deceived her, and I knew she shouldn't even be talking to me. But I had just scored, only I didn't know what to do with the information. I supposed Althea Goodman's scholarship had gotten him to Wharton, and I had a brief moment of unselfish gratitude that she had lived to see that.

I knew that Wharton was a very private and very prestigious school of business at the University of Pennsylvania. A call to Wharton was almost unproductive—the alumni relations person merely confirmed that he received an MBA. He was not allowed to tell me any more than that.

Stumped, I decided to get dressed for that lunch I didn't want to go to. My idea of "dressed" was a pair of clean jeans, without artful holes, and an oversize pullover out of French terry. Should be good enough for one of the local coffee shops.

Back at my computer, I decided to start with an internet search of all the usual places—Facebook, Twitter, Instagram, and so on. That took about fifteen minutes because, not at all to my surprise, Howard showed up on none of them. I needed a business search. The Chicago Athletic Association was a long shot but could be important—that exclusive, men-only club closed in 2005, but Howard could conceivably have landed in Chicago in '97 or '98. I couldn't find any membership records online, and the association was now a swanky hotel. I doubted they would know.

If I were an ambitious businessman newly come to Chicago and wanted to associate with the rich and powerful, of which Chicago has always had plenty, I'd join the downtown branch of Rotary. Eureka! Membership records showed that Howard affiliated in '98. But of course, nothing told me what kind of business he was in. Was he employed or independent? I considered throwing the computer across the room.

A soft knock on the door prevented me. I called out, "Come in," and Madison sailed into my kitchen.

"You ready for lunch?" She wore leggings and a crisply starched white peasant's shirt. And she looked smashing, her hair loose around her face, her makeup perfect. Oh darn! I'd forgotten makeup when I dressed.

"Sure. Just let me powder my nose." And that's literally what I did—dabbed a bit of powder on my nose, forgot about eye makeup, pinched my cheeks as though I were a proper nineteenth-century lady. My hair, too, was loose around my face, but somehow the effect wasn't the same.

Since Maddie didn't know the neighborhood, I had a couple of suggestions—the Harper Café because it was on-campus, where she'd be going, or Café 53 on Fifty-Third Street, which had awesome sandwiches. I made these suggestions as I loaded my purse with keys and lipstick and a credit card.

"Oh, Henny, I thought we'd go to the restaurant at the Sophy Hotel. I'm thinking of staying there while I look for an apartment."

One of my problems is that I'm always practical—translate into penny-pinching. The other is that I'm fairly outspoken. Both came into play. "The Sophy?" I blurted out. "Maddie, it's a boutique hotel. Expensive."

"I know," she said, "but it looks safe and comfortable. And I want to check it out. No problem. Lunch is my treat."

I protested long and loud enough to be polite, but we were going to the Sophy on Fifty-Third. And we were going in her car, which proved to be a new red Jeep Wrangler. I was beginning to feel like the poor cousin and had a fleeting thought that maybe that's what Patrick really was.

The Sophy proved to be everything I'd heard—small and elegant with a waitstaff that almost but not quite hovered. Maddie ordered a margarita, so I felt free to have a glass of wine. When the waiter hurried away, I searched my brain for Maddie's field of study.

"If you're looking for an apartment, I gather you got the fellowship. Congratulations." Art. That was it, Art history. I took a chance. "Art history, isn't it?"

"Close," she laughed. "Architecture. I want to combine it with the Chicago studies program and focus on Chicago architecture. You know, Daniel Burnham and the effects of the Chicago Fire on modern architecture."

No, I didn't know. I knew Hyde Park had some Frank Lloyd Wright homes, including Robie House on the university campus, but I'd only heard the name Burnham somewhere, didn't know a thing about him. So, feigning deep interest, I asked.

"You know, the architect of the Columbian Exposition, and really the man who laid out the plan for a rebuilt Chicago after the Great Fire. Burnham was responsible for the first building given the name of skyscraper, and he literally planned Chicago. Urban planning will be a big part of my study. I'm excited about it."

It sounded deadly dull to me, but then I supposed cooking bored Maddie. So there we were, studying the menu. Maddie chose the lobster roll, and I figured if the hostess chose the most expensive thing on the menu, I could too.

While we waited, I found out sort of what lunch was about. "I'm so glad you moved in next to Patrick," she said. "I've been worried about him. Waiting for him to find the right girl."

That sinking feeling was my stomach dropping down into my toes. She didn't know her cousin, her beloved Paddy, was gay! "Oh well," I said, struggling, "you know some people take longer than others to settle down."

"I know, but he's so sweet and kind. And I think he's good-looking. But he never has had many girlfriends, so I'm delighted to see how much he likes you."

"Well, thanks. I . . . like him a lot too. And I agree with you, he's good-looking." I did not want to get into a corner where I'd have to give Maddie an unwelcome explanation.

"What are your future plans?" she asked brightly. "Are you planning a career in television or do you really want to be a chef?"

Thanks goodness—another direction. I prattled on about my dream of managing the food segments on the *Today* show, which had gone from a spur-of-the-moment invention to something I now believed I really wanted, and told her just a little about my current job. The rest of the lunch we talked about architecture and culinary matters and managed to steer away from Patrick. But as she dropped me at my apartment, she said, "Please don't hurt Patrick."

What else could I say but, "Of course not."

I never did learn any more about Howard that afternoon, mostly because I'd lost heart for the hunt. His life between 1998 and 2019 remained a blank to me—twenty-one lost years. Even more, I had no idea where he got his money.

The only remarkable event that afternoon was that Irene called and wanted to know why I wasn't at the apartment.

"Howard told me to take a few days to plan menus, so I've been working at home."

"Howard does not run the show," she said crisply, the old Irene present in full force. "I'd like to see you up here tomorrow morning. Shall we say ten o'clock?"

"Yes, ma'am. I'll be there, as close to ten as the bus makes it." I wished that particular husband-and-wife team would talk to each other.

* * *

When Patrick came home that evening, I was waiting to pounce. He must have known because he walked right past my door, but I heard him and was in the hall before he could turn the key in his lock.

"Oh, hi, Henny."

"Hi, nothing. Patrick O'Malley, you get in here. You've got explaining to do."

That earned me a pained look and a stilted, "I have no idea what you're talking about."

"Your cousin, Maddie, that's who, not what. Do we have to stand here in the hall to talk about it?"

We settled at my kitchen table, and I demanded, "So are you the poor cousin from the wrong side of the tracks? Maddie treated me to lunch at the Sophy today—a lobster roll, with a glass of wine. I can't afford to eat like that! And she tells me she's going to stay at the Sophy while she looks for an apartment."

He grinned. "Is that all? Yes, she does come from a bit of money. Her dad's a lawyer in Winnetka. He, ah, does very well. And no, I'm not from the wrong side of the tracks. My dad's a CPA and my mom teaches English at the college level. We just don't have Maddie's kind of money."

It was time for me to grudgingly make a confession. "Maddie doesn't act like she has money," I began. "I mean, she's nice, and I like her. It's just if I'd have known ahead of time, I'd have had a whole different mindset about lunch, and I'd have worn better clothes."

"You look fine. Is there something else, or can I go now?" He stood.

I stared at him. Yes, there was something else, but how could I tell him Maddie was worried about him and wanted a full admission that I was his girlfriend. How could I tell him she didn't understand about him?

"Go on," I said. "I have to get back to tracing Howard. So far, I've got a twenty-one-year gap with no idea what he did . . . or does."

He sat back down. "Tell me what you found."

I did, and he listened attentively to all of it—the Wharton School of Business, even Rotary. "I bet he was in Paris when Gabrielle was born. Come to think of it, you ought to see what you can find about Irene. She might lead you to Howard."

"And Gabrielle might lead me to Irene," I mused.

"Careful of that one, Henny." And he was gone.

That evening I composed a careful note that I would try to slip to Gabrielle when I was at the apartment tomorrow. It simply said, "Call me when you can talk. I have questions."

Chapter Eleven

I never did get to give Gabrielle that note. Next morning, when I got off the bus near the Foxglove apartment, I saw a cluster of police cars, an ambulance, a fire truck, and a small crowd of spectators, but I paid no attention because they seemed to all be focused on a building two doors down from my destination. None of my business, and I was already a bit late for Irene's arbitrary ten o'clock command performance.

But as I reached for the apartment building door, a hand grabbed my arm, rather rudely, from behind, and a man demanded, "Where do you think you're going?"

I turned and pulled my arm free. "To my employer's apartment," I said with as much hauteur as I could manage—not an easy attitude for me. "And I'm late."

"Who is your employer?"

It had finally dawned on me that he had on a police uniform, and I was beginning to be a bit intimidated. "Irene Foxglove."

"Come with me," he said, taking my arm again and almost dragging me away.

I reminded myself briefly of a dog I had when I was young. If Sophie didn't want to go someplace on the leash, she'd dig all four feet into the ground and pull back, like a stubborn mule. It worked better for her than it now did for me.

Impatiently, he said, "We're going to that police car over there, so you can wait for the detective, who will want to question you."

Panic set in and my stomach did that drop-to-my-boots thing again. "Wait! What's happened? Is someone hurt? You've got to tell me." By then I was pleading.

"Your employer's husband has had an accident. He's dead. We think it was an accident, but with sudden, unexpected death, we have to cover all possibilities."

"Howard? Dead?" It came out as a hoarse whisper.

For the first time, the police officer showed a little compassion. He was the opposite of Patrick, though younger—dark hair cut in a burr, dark brown eyes that had no laughter in them at this moment, and a sort of tight mouth. Still, he was good-looking in his own way, and I had the thought, inappropriate to the moment, that I would never introduce him to Patrick.

"I have to get to Irene. She'll need me."

"Her daughter is with her." His voice was gentler now.

"That will only make things worse," I blurted out and then wished for that message that says, "Henny James would like to withdraw that last comment."

"You better explain that to the detective," he said, steering me toward the car and unceremoniously pushing me into the back seat.

I waited. Each time I checked my watch, convinced I'd been in that car an hour, I'd find it was barely five minutes since the last time I checked. Finally, a man in a suit crawled in to sit beside me, and I had yet another panicky thought: maybe this was a murderer masquerading as a detective. He wasn't my mental image of a detective. Probably in his late forties, he was almost bald—headed in that direction, and a bit overweight—headed there too. He looked tired, and he smelled of stale cigarettes. I asked him to open the car window regardless of the cool breeze coming off the lake.

He must have read my mind, because he flashed a badge. "Detective Al Schmidt. Just a few questions."

I had the first one. "What happened?"

"Looks like he stumbled and hit his head on the edge of a concrete step. Probably died instantly. Tell me why you were headed to his apartment."

I did, and the following questions were predictable—did I like Howard? Trust him? That sort of thing. Until he came to the part where he questioned my arrival time. Seems he thought it possible that I had come earlier, pushed Howard down, left, and come back again on the bus.

"Sir, have you ever tried to take public transportation from Hyde Park to the North Shore?"

He admitted he hadn't. And I said if he had, he'd realize how ridiculous that suspicion was.

"Why did you tell an officer that Gabrielle Foxglove would not help her mother right now?"

So my friendly officer had ratted me out! "Because it's true. They do not get along. Gabrielle is terribly spoiled, and Irene is not by nature a warm, loving person."

"Was Gabrielle closer to her father?"

Dilemma. Shouldn't the detective find out all this for himself? On the other hand, should I lie to protect Gabrielle? Reluctantly, I told the truth: "Howard is . . . was her stepfather. She doesn't know her biological father." No need to tell him she wanted me to find that mystery man.

"Okay. I repeat, did they get along?"

"Not really. Howard was a patient and gentle man, but Gabrielle resented him. She's been spoiled all her life, and she thinks she can have whatever she demands. Howard didn't go along with that, though Irene was often ready to do whatever she thought would keep the peace."

Detective Schmidt began to backtrack, asking me over again questions that he'd already asked, checking, I guess, to see if my story would change. No longer intimidated, I was tired of him and worried about Irene.

"Detective, are we almost through? Mrs. Foxglove needs me."

"Needs you? Are you her support system?"

Oh, for heaven's sake. I was not going to get into psychoanalysis. "I'm her assistant."

Finally, he said, "You're free to go, though if things change, we may want to talk to you again."

"You have my address and phone number." Things change? What was going to change? Howard was dead. That was it.

He got out of the car and motioned to that same nameless policeman, who came to escort me to the Foxglove apartment, and, I guess, guarantee that I was "approved." A grim policewoman stood at the door and nodded solemnly when the officer said I could see "the widow." That phrase hit me like a ton of bricks.

The widow was seated at the same conference-cum-dining table where we planned everything from shows to a cookbook. As I approached, I could see how rigid her spine was, and I knew she was holding herself together by willpower. Her left arm lay heavily in her lap, while the fingers of her right hand gave away her stress by tapping on the table. I bet her left hand was twitching in that cast. Her hair was neatly done, and I bet when she turned toward me, I'd see makeup on that face.

But when she turned, the usually distant Irene bowled me over with a hug so ferocious and long that I nearly landed on the Oriental rug. "Thank God," she said, pulling back so that I now saw the tracks of tears spoiling her makeup. Little rivulets of mascara ran down both cheeks, and she wiped at them with a crumpled Kleenex.

Gabrielle sat halfway down the table—not close to her mother's seat—and lounged indolently in her chair, slouched so that she sat on the end of her tailbone, her back almost curved into a question mark. "Welcome, Henny. Glad you could join us."

I threw her what I hoped was a dirty look, and turned to deal with Irene, who was now asking, "Where have you been? I've been asking for you. You were supposed to be here at ten—almost an hour and a half ago." Even in grief, she couldn't forget her control over me.

"I've been downstairs, a captive of a detective named Schmidt. He seemed to think I might have killed Howard. Oh, Irene, I am so sorry." And now I was the one who threw my arms around her.

"He thinks that about all of us," Gabrielle said laconically. "But it was an accident. Wasn't it, Mother dear?"

Irene ignored her. "I don't know what to do," she said, wiping at her face again until I wanted to fetch her a new tissue. "Howard was everything. I don't know how the show will go on. He made it all happen. He loved me very much"—was she convincing me or Gabrielle?—"and I loved him dearly. I . . . I don't know how I'll carry on."

I squeezed her free hand. This did not seem the time to tell her we couldn't do any more reruns, and the network had decreed we would have to tape come Monday evening—four days away.

She began to wail, a keening sound that cut through me. "How does a perfectly healthy man go out for a walk and end up dead? And why in the hell was he going for a walk at nine thirty in the morning? He never walked anywhere. Despised it." By now, she was speaking through sobs, tears flowing again.

I figured at this point all I could do was listen. Until I got a direct order, that is. Irene did one of her instant recoveries, straightening suddenly as though she'd just had a new thought. "Henny, it's almost lunchtime. Would you go see what's in the refrigerator and what you could whip up? I have no idea. Howard always handled our meals too."

A chef who didn't feed her own family. Knowing Irene, it was no surprise, but it made me realize even more how much Howard took care of her and how lost she would be without his protection. Was that my job now? "I'm on it," I said, rising from the table. I was clear in my own mind what I was on was lunch preparation, not the lifelong job of saving Irene.

For the non-cook he claimed to be, Howard kept a pretty well-stocked refrigerator. I found sliced chicken, obviously from one of those rotisserie stands at the grocery, along with tomatoes, eggs, cheeses, pickles. I pulled it all out and rummaged around until I found mayonnaise and sour cream and discovered lemons in the vegetable crisper. Don't ask. He must have had a reason. I was beginning to like Howard more, sorry that it was too late.

In the pantry, I found a can of tiny new potatoes and another of green beans plus a bag of croutons. Okay, it was going to be a weird Cobb salad, but I thought it would be good. Canned green beans?

I'd just whip up a creamy blue cheese dressing, boil some eggs, and lay it all out on a platter I found after looking in six cabinets.

I made the dressing while the eggs boiled, tasting as I went along, adding a little lemon juice, a little vinegar, some dry mustard, and, finally, chopped green onions. Some of Howard's groceries may have been utilitarian, but he had some darn good blue cheese and I thought the dressing was good.

Twenty minutes later, I carried the salad into the dining area and plopped it down with pride—except neither Irene nor Gabrielle seemed to notice.

"Gabrielle," I said sharply, "are there paper plates?"

Before she could answer, if she would have, Irene collected herself enough to announce, "I will not eat off paper."

I looked at Gabrielle, whose place I certainly thought it was to jump up with a cheery, "I'll get the plates."

Instead, she offered, "They're in the kitchen cabinet above the dishwasher."

Lunch was a silent affair. Gabrielle picked and played with her food, just as she had the night we met at Jimmy's. Irene ate a few bites, then pushed her plate back, and said, "I'm not hungry. I'll save it for later."

Irene made one suggestion that I refused to dignify with an answer. Beginning with, "I just don't know when I'll be able to work again," she asked, "What was the name of that woman who made such a fuss about cassoulet?"

Before I could say, "Ina Faye Clark," Irene added, "Maybe she'd do the show for a few weeks."

Now or never, I thought. "Irene, we don't know the status of the show. We don't really know how much it depended on Howard, but it could be we won't have a studio or a production channel. You'll have to call Howard's lawyer, preferably today. But one thing I do know is that the network will not let us continue to do reruns. They want fresh material. We've got to tape Monday. I've got the recipes all ready."

She gasped, but after a minute she asked, "What recipes?" And why hadn't she approved them?

That OxyContin must have been some strong stuff. "You did approve them. Remember, we're riffing off James Beard. Recipes for an American food cookbook. *Irene's Favorite Forty.*"

For a minute she looked like she'd never heard of the idea, but then she slowly smiled. "Yes. Can I do that?"

Was she asking me? "Yes, you can."

Gabrielle had remained quiet, but now she said, "Give it a try, Mother. If you fall on your ass, I'll call Ina Faye Clark."

Detective Schmidt walked in, unannounced. "Mrs. Foxglove? We're packing it up now."

She turned, haughtily in command now. "Where is my husband?"

I'm sure I gasped, but she sounded like she expected him at any minute for a late lunch. Schmidt was gentle, I'll give him that.

"Ma'am, when there is a sudden death, without a physician in attendance, we are required by law to do an autopsy. We'll notify you when we're ready to release the body."

"Oh, my! Howard wouldn't like that. Not at all. Your officer"— she nodded in the direction of the uniformed woman—"said you were quite satisfied that he fell and hit his head. I see no necessity for anything further."

He took a deep breath, rubbed his hand across his balding head, opened and shut his mouth. Finally, he said, "In working the scene, we found some things that, ah, concerned us."

"Concerned?"

"We believe there was a confrontation. There is some evidence of defensive wounds."

That was my first hint that things were really about to go south. I glanced at Gabrielle, but she remained impassive. And I suddenly wanted Patrick's good sense to get me out of here.

What with doing the dishes—Gabrielle disappeared into the bedrooms—and worrying about how safe Irene would or wouldn't be if I left, I missed my usual bus and caught the five-thirty one, which meant I was crossing from almost one end of the city to the other in the midst of rush hour. It was pushing seven when I got to my building.

Chapter Twelve

I barely stopped to open my door, put my purse on the table, and kick off my shoes. Then I padded barefoot to Patrick's door and raised my hand to knock. I must have made more noise than I thought, because just as I leaned toward the door for the knock, he opened it. Momentum carried me forward, and I flew into the apartment—and into Patrick, knocking him flat and landing on top of him. Awkward, to say the least. And when I looked around in that split second, I saw that his head had just barely missed an end table.

Scrambling off him, I cried, "That's just how Howard died!"

Blinking in confusion, Patrick sat up, rubbed his neck, and inquired politely, "Henny, what the hell are you talking about?"

The perfect man swore! I'd never heard him do that before. Instead of answering, I said, "Maybe it really was murder."

"Murder?" he echoed. "You almost murdered me, but what are you blabbering about Howard?" By now, I guess Patrick felt he knew Howard, even though they'd never met.

"Howard's dead," I said solemnly.

"Be serious, Henny. What's going on?"

"Honest. He's dead."

So then I had to tell him the whole story, the two of us sitting there, cross legged as though we were on a campout. As I related the day's events, I swung back and forth between tears and hysteria-induced giggles. I suspect when the latter happened, he wanted to slap some sense into me. I ended the whole story with, "I really don't like Gabrielle."

"Yeah, I gathered. Now what?"

"I don't know. I just don't know. How was your day? Are the stars aligning?"

"Don't change the subject. You obviously can't just walk away from this—you have shows to tape, and if I hear you right, you're a tad worried about Irene's safety."

"A big tad," I said and put my head in my hands and sobbed.

Patrick did what I always half-wanted him to. He put his arms around me, let me cry on his shoulder, and stroked my hair, murmuring soft reassurances. In spite of my grief, I cursed the gay gods. Why him?

Suddenly moving away, he got to his feet and pulled me up. "I know what you need," he announced. "Chinese takeout. And you will walk with me to get it."

"It's almost dark," I protested.

"I'll keep you safe. And it's only on Fifty-Seventh and Dorchester. A walk will clear your head."

We got vegan vegetable rolls, Pad Thai Noodles, Lo Mein, and Pepper Steak, a veritable feast, plus sticky white rice, all in those little containers that Chinese places still use. Back at the apartment, Patrick produced a good sauvignon blanc, to my delight, because even though we were having Chinese, not Japanese, I was afraid he'd want sake, which I really don't care for.

We gorged, and we drank, and I almost but not quite forgot about Irene, and Howard, and Gabrielle. We laughed and giggled, and the last I remember, Patrick guided me to my bed, threw a blanket over me, and said, "See you in the morning. Sweet dreams." The combination of exhaustion and liquor had rendered me beyond caring, and I think I mumbled, "G'night."

By all that's holy, I should have slept till noon and wakened with cotton in my mouth and a jackhammer in my head. That's not what happened—at least not quite. I wakened at four in the morning. Sat straight up in bed with a clear conviction that Irene was in danger—and I needed to protect her. I guess adrenaline kicked in because only when I sat on the edge of the bed and leaned down for my slippers did the jackhammer start. I immediately went back to bed, but sleep was beyond me.

I couldn't call Irene at four in the morning. But what if she really needed me? Was I having some kind of paranormal experience, or was my imagination working overtime? Four in the morning is probably the worst time to ask yourself deep questions or to let your mind wander. Because my mind wandered far and wide. The killer had come back to finish his job. She had gone out to look at the murder site and had herself fallen, just like Howard did. Gabrielle had poisoned her—somehow, I couldn't see Gabrielle using physical violence, but I could easily imagine her with poison.

I watched the clock: five, then six. Finally seven o'clock, when light barely began to streak the sky over what I couldn't quite see from my apartment but knew was Lake Michigan. Seven was the earliest I thought it respectable or practical to get out of bed. It was still too early to call Irene, though I did laugh at myself. Sure that she had been killed in the night, I was still afraid of waking her. Coffee didn't help much.

Neither did Patrick, who stuck his head in the door on his way to class. The expression on his face was less concern than glee as he called out, "Morning, Sunshine." He expected to see me bleary-eyed, holding my aching head.

Determined to surprise him, I gave him back as cheerful a "Morning" as I could manage.

"How're you feeling?" He was pushing his luck.

"Medium, no thanks to you. Why did you let me drink so much wine?"

He shrugged. "I thought it might be good for you. Stop you from thinking about Howard."

I gave up on the brave front I was trying to present. "I'm worried about Irene."

"Of course you are." He stood in the doorway, impatient to be gone. "We always worry about someone who's lost a loved one."

Was that a pat speech he'd memorized from somewhere? "I don't mean that kind of worry." Now I could feel myself getting cranky. "I think something bad happened during the night, but I don't know what."

"Call her." He was literally standing on one foot and then the other, and the backpack he wore over one shoulder practically bounced.

"I don't want to wake her." I took a deliberate, slow sip of my coffee.

"Oh, for Pete's sake, Henny. Then just sit here and worry yourself sick. I've got an eight o'clock this morning." And he was gone.

I worried and stewed for another hour and finally, a bit after nine, called Irene. She sounded breathless. "Henny, I'm so glad you called. I wanted to call you, but I was afraid it was too early."

"Oh, I've been up for hours, Irene." Wonder if she caught the wry tone. "I'm starting on menus for our Monday taping." Well, I hadn't started yet but that was my intention for the day. I had the dishes chosen and all my notes, so it was just a matter of organizing. I thought that casual comment was a better start to the conversation than an anguished, "Are you all right? What's up?"

"Something *terrible* happened last night." She gave the word the French twist, and despite the beat my heart skipped, I wanted to tell her this was no time to sprinkle her conversation with French. If she's talking to me on the phone and throwing in *terrible*, which is a deliberate affectation on her part, nothing too terrible had happened. "What?"

"Someone, *a méchant*, a burglar, tried to get into our building last night. The alarm went off and scared him away."

Méchant was new to me but I got the meaning. "Did the police come?"

"*Oui.* They said it was strange that whoever targeted our building, since we"—her voice broke just a bit—"had just had a death here. Poor Howard. I'm sure it had nothing to do with him. Just coincidence."

"Yeah," I mused aloud, "just coincidence, Madame." If she was feeling her French this morning, I'd cater to her, no pun intended. But I didn't believe it was a coincidence at all. I tried to think of reasons someone would break in—besides murdering Irene. Did Howard have something they wanted, perhaps papers? Perhaps even papers that would give away what appeared to be the big secrets in their lives: the source of Howard's money and the identity of Gabrielle's father. What if the two were one and the same?

Irene broke into my thoughts. "Henrietta! Are you still there? Why are you silent so long?"

"Sorry, Madame. Of course it was a coincidence. But I have a suggestion for you. Do you have a pencil and paper handy?"

"Just a minute." A pause, and then she was back. "I'm ready."

"Did you call Howard's lawyer yesterday, as I suggested? I think you need to make an immediate appointment with him." Somehow, I knew Howard's lawyer would be male, a corporate type. "You need his advice, and perhaps he can tell you if there's enough money in the will to continue the show and keep the apartment." A loud gasp from her made me grateful I was saying this over the phone, even though my fingers were cramping from holding my cell phone so tightly.

"The show makes money," she protested. "It does not cost us. Howard always told me it puts—how did he say it?—bread and bacon on our table. And the apartment—we own it. It could not be any other way. I am sure of all this. Howard always took good care of me."

I wasn't as sure as she was, but I didn't say that. Squirming uncomfortably in my chair, I said, "Just call and confirm all that. And, Madame, there is something else: I want you to go through Howard's desk, briefcase, dresser drawers—wherever you might find bank statements, insurance papers, any other financial records."

"*C'est trop!* It is too much. You will come help me, no?"

"No. I must prepare for Monday in the studio."

"Oh, the studio be bothered. I will not be there."

Was this the woman who just told me the show put the bread and bacon on the table? I didn't really believe the show did that, but she believed it. That made me assume she'd come to her senses over the weekend. I almost chided her with a cheery, "The show must go on!" Wonder how you say that in French? I ended the conversation by assuring Irene she could call me any time.

I didn't let go of the suspicious break-in, though. I wondered if Detective Schmidt would talk to me. I tried, and to my surprise, whoever answered put the call through and within seconds I heard him say, "Schmidt."

"Uh, Detective Schmidt." I stumbled a bit, uncertain of myself. "This is Henrietta James, Mrs. Foxglove's assistant. I was concerned about the break-in at her apartment building. She tells me it has nothing to do with her, just coincidence but—"

"I don't believe in coincidences." He broke in bluntly. "Tell me about your concern."

"Well, Howard's just dead . . ." I hesitated.

"And?"

It came out in a rush. "He told me he was worried about Irene. Said there had been threats."

"Mrs. Foxglove was definitely the object of last night's incident. The landlord told me that Mr. Foxglove had installed an under-the-carpet alarm in front of their door, with the landlord's permission. It was triggered last night and set off loud alarms inside the hallways and outside the building." All this was delivered in a staccato-like cadence. "Either Mrs. Foxglove is the target, or someone wants something that the decedent had in the apartment."

Well, nice to know that someone with more knowledge agreed with my suspicions, but it didn't get me any further toward knowing what to do. "Does Mrs. Foxglove know this?"

"No. I thought it best not to alarm her. We will put a twenty-four-hour guard at the building for a few days."

There went my Monday taping. "And if she leaves?"

"We can't protect her then."

"What can I do?"

"Keep your eyes and ears open. Call me if you have the least suspicion. Gotta go." And he hung up.

Still in the crumpled clothes I'd worn the night before, I piddled around the apartment, almost gagging at Chinese food that had sat out all night. I ate a bowl of cereal and was about to head for the shower and clean clothes when a loud, heavy banging on my door froze me where I stood. Clearly this was not Patrick—first of all, he was in class and second, he didn't knock—and it was not Maddie, because her knock was as gentle and ladylike as she was.

Hesitant and just a bit apprehensive, I made sure the chain was on the door and then called out to ask who it was.

"Penny," an unmistakable voice boomed. "Penny Aldrich. Let me in. We got business."

Slowly, I removed the chain, wondering how she knew where I lived. Of course, Irene probably called to tell her about Howard and shared my address. I wished she had asked me first.

"Come in." My reluctance crept into my voice.

You'd have thought we were in the apartment on North Clarendon, the way she barged in and slammed her briefcase on the table, nearly knocking my cereal bowl to the floor. "Too bad about Howard," she proclaimed, "but I never did cotton to him. Stingy bastard."

I was stunned. I'd been raised never to speak ill of the dead.

Spreading out papers, some of which looked like spreadsheets, she kept talking. "Now we can do the cookbook the way it should be done. Four color. Beautiful. We'll make a real star out of our girl."

In desperation, I said, "Let me make a fresh pot of coffee." I could think of nothing else useful.

"Fine. Now tell me about the recipes you've chosen—or Irene has."

The coffeemaker perked and bubbled as I said, "As you and I discussed, we've decided to do menus, instead of dishes. With an emphasis on what Americans can cook in their own kitchens. We'll play off James Beard and feature traditional American editions and a few adaptations. To please Irene I included a French menu—coq au vin, and she can make her beloved crème brûlée. I suspect we'll do a German meal—hot potato salad, sweet and sour red cabbage, maybe sausage or schnitzel."

"She hates Germans."

"She's still thinking of World War II, even though it was well before her time. I can talk her around that and around an Italian meal. But I think we'll skip Asian cooking completely." I rose and poured coffee, knowing Penny took hers black and strong. How typical!

"I can have a photographer in the studio Monday morning. I've already hooked up with one."

"Monday's a little iffy. First of all, we're taping in the late afternoon. And Irene says she has too much else to worry about. She won't be there."

That formidable head of gray hair swung back and forth as she made shook her head in the traditional negative way of saying "no." "Reruns won't do!" she almost shouted, and I was grateful Patrick was at school. "We're losing audience."

"Have you seen statistics?"

"No. But I just know. Been in this business a long time." She stood up, stretched, and began to pace, suddenly stopping to whirl and look at me. "Ina Faye Clark can tape the show. She wants to do it anyway, and this is the perfect opportunity."

An outrageous suggestion! "Ina Faye will not appear on Irene's show. Howard wouldn't allow it when he was alive, and I won't allow it now." My voice was firm and steady, thank goodness.

"Howard won't know, and you're just being silly. She can do the show, and the photographer can do food shots. We can dub in pictures of Irene later. Of course, I'll have to be in the studio. And I'll have to charge for my time. I don't do this for my health."

"Until we know about Howard's estate and the true status of the show, we're cutting expenses, not increasing them. And Ina Faye will not ever take Irene's place."

Before she thought, she burst out with, "But I promised her."

I stood, coming as close to eye level as I could. I hoped my voice and eyes were as cold as I felt. "Penny, are you working for Ina Faye too?"

She had the grace to hang her head momentarily. "I gotta make a living."

"Not by double-crossing Irene, you don't. You're fired!"

"You can't do that! Howard hired me."

"And regretted it. Do you have a written contract to show me?" I nodded toward the briefcase.

"No." It was almost a whisper.

"Then get out." For drama, I marched around the table and opened the apartment door.

Muttering about calling Irene and taking me to court, she scrabbled together her papers, stuffed them blindly into her briefcase, and left, passing within an inch of me but with her head lowered to avoid my eyes.

After I slammed the door shut, hard, I sank into my chair at the table, drained of all my energy but also of my indignation. It was like the negative emotions had gone out the door with Penny. I'd have to call Irene, but I'd deal with that later.

And Penny had left me with one very unwelcome thought: I would be taping Monday's show—and who knows how many after that.

* * *

My mother chose that moment to call. "Henny, dear, I know it's not Sunday, but I just had this strange feeling that you need me. Your father said I should get a plane ticket and get up there, but I thought I'd check with you first. Everything okay?"

Was being psychic suddenly running in the family? Her intuition aside, this was absolutely the wrong time for Mom to come charging up here. Blast! My dad should have checked with me before he mentioned planes and visits. Making my voice as cheery as I could I sang out, "I'm just fine, Mom. How about you?"

"I'd be a lot better if I weren't worrying about you. You know, Henny, there's a good culinary school in San Antonio if that's what you really want to do."

"There's an excellent one in Chicago, too," I said drily. "I'm just too wrapped up in my job right now." I meant that literally.

"Well, I would feel so much better if you were back in Texas. I don't like it that you don't seem to have made many friends besides that Patrick boy. And you seem stuck on hold there."

If you only knew, Mom, if you only knew. "I've told you. Patrick and I are friends. Right now, my focus is on my work. That's how I want it."

"Well, I'm soon going to have to come up there to see for myself. And you will come home for Christmas, won't you?"

Christmas! I hadn't even thought about it. "Of course I'll try, Mom." Who knew what would unravel by Christmas?

Finally, she seemed reassured, and we ended the conversation. I thought, not for the first time, that my good old Methodist mom was the perfect fit for the stereotype of a Jewish mother.

Chapter Thirteen

My plan to devote the remainder of the week—one whole day—to planning for next week's shoot didn't quite work out as I hoped. Goaded by my conscience, I called that same evening to check on Irene. I had mentally prepared my rationale for firing Penny, but it seems I didn't need to break that news. Penny had called Irene as soon as she left my apartment. Irene's only comment was, "I told her you were handling my affairs in Howard's absence." She made it sound like his absence was only temporary, but I knew better, and a great weight settled on my shoulders.

"Frankly, I was weary of her, Henrietta, and I'm grateful you had more courage than poor Howard. Now we can do that cookbook the way we want." Where had I heard those words before?

Irene reported that the "man who takes care of this building"— I suspected that translated to owner—had someone come out to strengthen all locks and upgrade an alert system that. "There was one in the building. It went off the other night, and my goodness it was loud., But now it will also notify police directly. I feel quite safe.

And John Wilson will be here at ten tomorrow morning. I expect you to be here too."

"Who?" I had no idea who John Wilson was, nor did I want to lose a day to finding out.

"Howard's lawyer, of course."

"Madame, discussions between a lawyer and a client are privileged. He would object to my being there, and I have too much to do for next week's tapings."

"You don't still plan to tape Monday, do you? I told you I won't be there." Her tone was sharp.

"I may have to do the cooking myself." As the words slipped out of my mouth, I suddenly considered them brilliant. She couldn't stand competition. She would be there.

But not without protest. I heard a dramatic sigh over the phone and then, "First that Ina Faye woman and now you. I know how Julius Caesar must have felt."

It was all I could do to keep from laughing. Irene and poor old Julius. She was playing to my Marc Antony. I kept my tone level. "We do not have any more relevant tapes to run. We need new shows the week after next."

"Run irrelevant tapes," she snapped. "I'll see you in the morning."

As I hung up, I thought, *No, you won't. If I'm handling your affairs, I'm going to do what is best in my judgment. I won't be dictated to.*

But it wasn't Irene who called me. It was the unknown John Wilson himself. "Miss James? This is John Wilson, lawyer for the late Howard Foxglove."

I responded appropriately, wondering why on earth he was calling me.

"I think you should meet with Mrs. Foxglove and me in the morning. That detective—Schmidt, I believe—has told her she is a person of interest. And he wants her to identify the body tomorrow at one o'clock. I suspect she'll need you to go with her."

I nearly dropped the phone. I was willing to do a lot for Irene but looking at Howard's body was not on the list. "Why? They know it's him, don't they? Do they think he had a double? A twin?" A realization kicked in. "Person of interest? Are they talking murder?"

I remembered the detective had said there were concerns, but that was a far cry from murder.

I heard him sigh. "I'm afraid so. There apparently was some sort of struggle. They can tell from bruises on the body, skin under the fingernails that was not his—he scratched whoever he was fighting with. We've got a witness who saw two men, so we know he was not alone."

A witness? "Can the witness identify the other man?"

He gave a wry chuckle. "Nope. She's elderly and has cataracts. We're lucky she could tell it was two men and not double vision. We think the other man, whoever he was, pushed Mr. Foxglove so that he fell and hit his head."

I was floored. Without a word I walked to the couch and sank down. My mouth went dry, and my heartbeat jumped. This couldn't be happening. So that's what the detective meant when he referred to a confrontation. Sort of an understatement, I thought.

"Miss James, are you there?"

"Yes," I managed. "Just stunned. If the police know all that, why do they need Irene to look at the body. Do they want to show her the bruises?"

"I'm not a criminal lawyer, so I can only guess. If she's a person of interest, which really means a suspect, they want to see how she'll react to seeing his body. I'm not too concerned, because the spouse is almost always the first suspect. But as Howard repeatedly told me, his wife is highly emotional. I think your presence might calm her."

"Does she know all this? That Howard was in a confrontation. And how can she be a suspect if that woman saw another man?"

"She's not officially a suspect—yet. But, I assume the police want to eliminate the possibility that she hired the other man. She did not show much emotion, certainly not the hysterics the police expected. That made them want to look more closely at her. I'll try to instruct her tomorrow."

"And it's legal for me to be there when you talk to her?"

"She requested it. She is not used to handling her own affairs, and I think she is like an airline passenger—she wants to know someone capable is flying the plane."

"Where . . . where is Howard now?" It seemed an awkward question to me. I didn't want to say, "the body," and yet I knew they wouldn't have just kept him at the local police station.

That slight chuckle again. "The viewing will be at the Cook County morgue on West Harrison."

This whole conversation only increased the burden I felt on my shoulders. Nonetheless, I was beginning to like this guy. I'd worry tomorrow about how to find the morgue. "I'll be there, but can you push the meeting to ten thirty? The bus doesn't get me there until after ten."

"Where are you coming from?"

"Hyde Park."

"I'll send a driver. Give me the address."

Really? I gave it to him, heard his computer keys clicking, and then heard, "His name will be Benjamin. He won't be in uniform, but he'll have ID to show you. See you tomorrow." And he was gone.

* * *

Benjamin proved to be a tall, slim black man of indeterminate age and graceful movements. He knocked on my apartment door at promptly nine thirty. I answered as quickly as I could, but Patrick beat me and stood in the hall in almost an aggressive stance, asking "Help you?"

Benjamin grinned. "I'm to drive Miss Henrietta to the Foxglove apartment. Here." He pulled out a laminated card identifying him as staff with the law firm of Wilson, Wilson, and Jones.

Patrick looked a question at me, and I reassured him. "Benjamin, meet Patrick O'Malley. I was expecting Benjamin, Patrick."

"Oh, okay, if you're sure." He disappeared inside.

"Let me get my purse," I said and grabbed purse, briefcase, sunglasses, and a Yeti.

Benjamin drove a modest gray limo. I headed to the passenger seat, but Benjamin pointedly held open the back door. I considered. I wanted to pick his brain a bit, but I wasn't sure I could do it from the back. I guess he read my mind.

"There's a communication system. I'll answer any questions you might have." Slight smile, but this guy was pretty impassive.

I sat in back. After he pulled away from the curb, Benjamin said, "Your first time to meet Mr. Wilson?"

For a fleeting moment I thought he was asking if it was my first time to ride in a limo. How embarrassing it would have been to have admitted that? Instead, my "yes" was confident.

He launched into a slight history, and by the time we were halfway downtown on Lake Shore Drive I knew that Mr. Wilson's late father, Richard, had founded the law firm and had handled Howard's affairs for many years. John had only taken over in the last six years. The firm now had twenty-four lawyers but no branch offices. They remained firmly anchored to downtown Chicago, with offices on Upper Wacker Drive, just inside the Loop.

There was so much I couldn't ask Benjamin without invading his professional relationships—what did he know about Howard personally? What had Mr. Wilson ever said to him about Irene? Did he know anything about Gabrielle's parentage? With those questions whirling in my mind, I spent the rest of the trip staring at the lake, which, being a Texas girl, always mesmerized me. I remembered the first time I saw it and spoke before I thought, saying, "You can't see the other shore." This day the lake was in one of its wild moods, whitecaps crashing against rocky shores and rolling deep onto beaches, the water a steel gray except in Burnham Harbor, where it remained blue and calm. The small planes parked at Meigs Field seemed to dance in the wind, and I was grateful for the solid security of Benjamin's limousine. Far out on its promontory, Shedd Aquarium stood, majestically impervious to the wind. I almost forgot about Irene and her problems, which were rapidly becoming my problems, and I was a bit surprised when Benjamin announced, "Here we are."

He came around, opened the door for me, and handed me a business card. "I am to drive you and Mrs. Foxglove to the coroner's office this afternoon. You shouldn't be there long, and I'll wait, bring Mrs. Foxglove back up here, and then take you home, if you don't mind all that traveling."

"I'll be grateful," I said, and he flashed me a slight smile as he opened the outer door to the apartment building. Looking for signs of forced entry, I saw none and used the key Howard had given me for the inner door. It didn't work. Of course, the locks had been changed. I rang the Foxglove button, and Irene buzzed the door open. Only then did Benjamin return to his car.

Irene met me at the door and, wordless and looking grim, led me to the dining table, where she had put out fresh coffee with real cream, little cubes of sugar, and tongs for grasping the cubes. A plate of croissants sat on the table.

"I had to send out for those first thing this morning," she complained.

Of course. She would never run such an errand herself; Gabrielle wouldn't do it, and she didn't think I'd get there in time or she would have sent me, even though I would have been afoot. Madame needed a housekeeper, I realized, and then almost let out an inadvertent giggle. Poor Howard—easily replaced by a housekeeper.

As if reading my mind, Irene said, "Without Howard, I'm going to need some help around here. I think you should come stay in our guest room, at least until things are sorted out."

Mentally I dug in my heels, even as my mind was thinking, "And leave Patrick?" Aloud I said, "Madame, I can't do that. I have an apartment, a life. I'm your assistant for the TV show, not for your life." It sounded harsh, and I wanted to recall the words the minute they left my lips.

She looked startled but didn't reply at first. Just stared at me until I was uncomfortable. Then, abruptly, she turned and said, "I need some help. Lord knows Gabrielle is no good." She looked at her watch and asked sharply, "Where is that lawyer?"

If I could have produced him somehow, I would have. Instead, I poured my coffee, conscientiously ignored the cream and sugar, and reached for a croissant. I had just taken the first bite when the buzzer sounded.

John Wilson was a slight, chipper man not much taller than I. Irene towered over him, but that didn't bother him. "Sorry I'm late. Decided to walk from the apartment, and it was farther than I calculated." He checked the time and announced, as if we didn't know, "Only ten minutes. Not bad. And now I feel quite refreshed after a walk on this brisk day!"

Then he seemed to remember his manners, dropping his briefcase on the floor and rushing toward Irene, both hands extended to reach for her hands. "I'm so sorry for your loss. Howard was a good man."

Instead of letting him take her hands, Irene stepped back, leaving him sort of awkwardly floundering in midair. He handled it with grace, turning toward the coffeepot and helping himself. Tight-lipped, Irene sat down without even a thank you.

He turned to me, "John Wilson, Henrietta. I am so very glad to meet you." I took the extended hands in mine, winced, and said, "Call me Henny. Everyone does."

Madame frowned.

"Well, let's get started." He was a bit too hearty, but it was a good cover for the awkward moment. He pulled out a leather portfolio with a clean legal pad on the clipboard and a thick collection of papers in the pocket. But he talked without looking at the papers, and the entire morning, he never took a note on that clipboard.

"Mrs. Foxglove, I want to assure you that Howard left you in good circumstances. He was, over the years, quite successful."

I wanted to interrupt with "Successful at what?" but I kept quiet. Something was bothering me, though, something about money. Did John Wilson know where Howard's money came from? Did he really know how much Howard was or wasn't worth?

"Several years ago he established a trust for you so that you would be well cared for. Gabrielle gets an outright, small inheritance, but you are free to supplement that as you wish."

Where was Gabrielle anyway? She ought to go to work was my opinion. No one asked or even looked at me. Irene was staring at the table, her mouth a tight slash across her face.

It took John, as he asked us to call him, most of the morning to give us the bare legal facts. He didn't actually read the will to us but promised a formal reading soon. Gabrielle would have to be present for that. He was authorized to advance Irene living expenses. She would not own the apartment but had a long-term lease. Eventually the landlord could raise the rent but not soon.

My mind wandered again toward all the unanswered questions but snapped back to attention as John said, "TV show."

"It was Howard's wish that the show continues as long as you wish to do it."

I nearly jumped out of my chair when Irene said, "I have no wish to continue it." Just as I was about to babble about the folly of decisions made in haste, John said, "I'm afraid you're under contract for another ten months. You are legally obligated."

I hoped my sigh of relief wasn't audible. It occurred to me I was here because he thought I would help Irene but all I was thinking about was myself and my opinions. I resolved to pay closer attention, but John seemed forthright and honest, and Irene had neither objected nor questioned anything he said until it came to the show. And at least he'd been firm about that—now she'd have to show up Monday. Or so I thought.

It was nearing noon when the buzzer sounded again. John immediately stood and announced, "I've taken the liberty of ordering lunch for us. My treat, of course."

A uniformed delivery person brought in our lunch—four Salad Niçoise. Wilson must have been catering to Irene's Gallic tendencies, and I wondered if he did it with tongue in cheek. Gabrielle's salad went into the refrigerator, since she did not appear, and Irene seemed to have no interest in calling her. We ate quietly. No doubt Irene was dreading the next step in our day as much as I was. They can call it whatever they want, but in my book, a morgue by any other name is still grim.

John wrapped things up quickly, checking his watch. "Benjamin will be here any minute. Irene, do you have any questions?"

Finally, she spoke. "Why do I have to identify Howard's body? I can give them a picture."

He sat down abruptly and fixed her with a hard look she could not avoid. "I'm going to be truthful with you. The police always suspect the spouse first in cases of murder. I believe we talked of this yesterday."

Her response was wooden. "I did not kill Howard, and I didn't hire someone to kill him. I loved him."

For a brief second I thought I saw a shadow pass across her eyes, and I wondered at her attitude. Where were the hysterics of two days ago? She didn't seem to be grieving, at least not outwardly. But she was hiding something.

John went on. "The police don't really need you to identify the body. That's a formality. But they want to watch your reaction. I would think it best if you could show some emotion, but not too much. No hysterics but sadness, grief. It will be unpleasant but brief."

I thought he was giving her a stiff assignment, but she just nodded. And I reminded myself that when she put her mind to it, Irene was a consummate actress.

"Henrietta, you will be with me?"

I gulped. "Yes, Madame."

And that's how I came to visit the offices of the Cook County Medical Examiner.

Chapter Fourteen

The Cook County morgue is on West Harrison, a bit west of the Loop, in a gray concrete building with deeply recessed small windows, the kind of utilitarian municipal architecture that sprang up across the country in the 1950s and '60s. Three flags flew on tall poles in front of the building—I recognized the Stars and Stripes, of course, but Benjamin had to identify the flags of Illinois and Cook County. It never occurred to me that a county could have its own flag, Irreverently, I wondered if they should be at half-mast in this place of death.

On the drive from the North Clarendon apartment, Benjamin had told us we shouldn't say morgue—the term was not in favor, although he didn't offer a good alternative. And there is no coroner, he said. The proper name of the office is Cook County Medical Examiner. Only it is four physicians in a group practice, which seemed logical to me. One coroner—oops, examiner—would be hard put to service all of Cook County.

Benjamin surprised me again with his brief, informative lectures, like the one on Wilson, Wilson, and Jones that he'd delivered earlier that morning. I was glad for a little advance information about this looming visit, but Irene had no interest at all in Benjamin's words. She stared out the window, and I wondered if she were girding herself for the encounter with death.

Benjamin left us at the front entrance, assuring us he'd be waiting, and he didn't think we'd be long. At the reception desk, I got to do all the talking—no surprise there. Irene stood by as though perhaps English were a foreign language and she was waiting for someone to break into French.

A man in scrubs, whose identification badge read Jerry Cobb and had his picture, came to lead us to the basement where that room with the unmentionable name was. He showed us into a small waiting room, its walls of cinder block painted a pale green, its furniture strictly office warehouse—chrome legs and arms on the chairs and a couch cushioned with foam rubber covered in scratchy tweed. Not a room where you'd want to linger. The tech assured us he'd be right back, and we sat in silence.

No surprise that Detective Schmidt joined us. "Want to verify your identification," he said briefly. Irene just nodded, and I remembered John Wilson's words. The detective came to see how Irene reacted to see, uh, Howard—dead.

Conversation lagged. Irene was self-absorbed, and the detective and I had nothing to say to each other. The minutes ticked by far too slowly.

Finally, the technician—or whatever his title was—returned, with what looked like hospital gowns, disposable head coverings, and booties. "Which of you is Mrs. Foxglove?" He looked from Irene to me, but I thought he must know the answer and it was a rhetorical question. Perhaps another part of protocol I didn't understand.

She was terse. "I am."

"Please put these on. I'll be glad to help you." And he did, putting the booties on while she sat on the couch, tucking her hair into the cap. Meanwhile, Schmidt struggled into similar disposable garments. Then the tech said, "This way, please" and the three of them left. Irene threw me a pleading glance, which I knew meant "Aren't you coming with me?"

Cobb said to me, "Your mother will be right back."

Great! That would go over so well with Irene. I certainly was not being the emotional support team I'd been designated.

Time slowed again, and I resisted the urge to pace, forcing myself to sit in that uncomfortable chair. They weren't gone long—just long enough for me to figure out what had been bothering me when John Wilson talked to us. The bank statements! Irene had not said a word about finding any papers in Howard's belongings that might give a clue about his financial life.

Irene came back alone, even more grim-faced, if possible. "It was Howard," she said matter-of-factly. "There was that birthmark." I was not about to ask where the birthmark was, but she sensed my curiosity. "Except for that I saw only his face. They said we could leave."

She stripped out of the protective gear. Detective Schmidt was nowhere to be seen, but Jerry Cobb was waiting at the reception desk. With professional distance, he said, "You can have a funeral home call at any time now to make arrangements. We ask that you do that as soon as possible." He didn't say it, but I heard in his words the warning that new bodies would be coming in, and it was a space problem—or a storage one.

In the car, she began talking . . . and then couldn't stop. "That was hard. I thought you would be with me. Hold my hand. You know, some comfort." It wasn't an accusation, just a statement. "There was poor Howard, his hair almost colorless and looking so thin on his head, his face a kind of mottled white." She buried her face in her hands, and I could see her shoulders shaking.

I really wanted to reach out and touch her, stroke a shoulder, somehow give her some human comfort. But, as Madame, she had always held herself aloof, and I was a bit intimidated. In conversation, even in cooking, I could match her and feel her equal, but we were in unknown territory here. One thing I knew for certain: this was not the time to ask about the bank statements.

Another thought that we couldn't discuss: was she really a suspect? What would Detective Schmidt do next? When would we hear? I didn't suppose it was like an exam, where the next day we'd get a pass or fail notice.

She finally fished around in her purse, looking for a tissue, and I silently held out a fresh pack I had specifically brought with us. As she wiped her eyes, her voice hardened again, and she said, "I will never forget that image. Howard will haunt me the rest of my life."

I hoped it wasn't true.

Irene's words to me as she got out of the car were, "I'll let you know when I am ready to return to the show. Meantime, you'll have to carry on."

At least she had gone from never returning to an indefinite date.

* * *

It was after three in the afternoon when Benjamin escorted me to the door of my apartment building. "Be sure to tell your neighbor you are home safely," he said with what for him seemed to be an unusual smile.

But I didn't knock on Patrick's door right away. I needed to collect myself. Was three o'clock too early for wine? Not after the day I'd had. I sat on the couch, nursing a glass of chardonnay and wishing, for the first time in a while, I had a dog. I needed someone to talk to.

Knocking on Patrick's door proved futile. He wasn't home. I wandered back into my apartment and then, on sudden impulse, picked up the phone and called John Wilson. To my surprise, the man answered his own phone with a terse, "John here." No secretary asking me to "Hold for Mr. Wilson." I liked him all the better.

"Henny! I'm glad to have a report. I've worried about you and Mrs. Foxglove all afternoon. How was it?"

I reported on her strange reaction, and he simply said, "She's a strange one, all right. Thank you for calling."

I thought he was about to hang up, so I quickly said, "John, there is something else. And I think you should know she does not like to be called Mrs. Foxglove. She prefers 'Madame.'"

Now there was outright laughter, and I could almost see tears running down his cheeks as he tried to control himself. "Sorry. Not appropriate on such an unhappy day, but I couldn't stop myself. I will remember your suggestion. Now, how may I help?"

"I'm wondering if Irene gave you Howard's bank statements or any business papers."

"No, but she wouldn't need to. His bank statements come to me electronically, and I'm pretty sure I have copies of all his papers."

"Might I look at the statements?" My mind scrambled to find a plausible reason and came up with, "I need to see if he was financing the show." Okay, the last was a little white lie.

"That's an unusual request and, frankly, as power of attorney it puts me in a difficult spot. The short legal answer is no, but I have other clients, and I can't spend a week going through those statements. I'd be grateful if you would and alert me to anything unusual. And I mean anything! I'll clear it with Irene and ask her to provide you with the copies she has, knowing I have backup, as does the bank of course."

My heart sank. Another bus trip up to the apartment, but John wasn't through. "I'll have a courier get them and any other papers from Irene and deliver them to you Monday."

My quick relief was overshadowed immediately. "Monday afternoon I'll be at the studio, taping a show." I didn't add "Alone," but he asked.

"Has Irene agreed to the taping?"

"No. I'm going solo. I'll say there's been a death in the family, and she'll return soon."

"I don't like the way this is going. I think Irene is keeping secrets. I hope you can uncover them." He paused a minute and then said, "Howard never discussed the arrangements of the show with me. I knew he was involved, but I know nothing of how it was financed. Now I'm curious."

"Me too."

I thought we were through, but he quickly said, "One other thing. Has Irene said anything to you about funeral arrangements or a funeral home?"

Dumb that I hadn't thought of it, but I hadn't. "Not a word. The medical examiner's office requested that the body be transferred to a funeral home as soon as possible. I guess they have a storage problem." Ghoulish thing to say. "But I just figured Irene would take care of it."

"I don't think she will," he said. "We've used a home in Wilmette before—none on the North Shore, needless to say. I'll handle that too under the guise of power of attorney."

My thoughts were a jumble as I hung up. How would I get Irene to tell me the truth? What was the truth? Did she really need protecting or was she maybe the most calculating, cold bitch in the world? I didn't really believe the latter, but she sure had been closed off from everyone since Howard's death. I knew one thing: I had to concentrate on the Monday taping. I dreaded the thought of doing it alone. In fact, the very idea unsettled my stomach, always a bad sign when dealing with food.

My computer reminded me that I had outlined two menus and really should have two more in mind. I was trying to balance beef and chicken, throw in a couple of seafood entrees and a smattering of French and Italian. I stared into space and finally remembered a dish called Shrimp Victoria—shrimp in a rich butter and sour cream sauce. And, somewhat cautiously, I added a tuna casserole. Irene would have a fit, but I thought it was time to update that much-scorned classic.

Deciding to do the shrimp and the hamburger Stroganoff dish for the next shows, I sketched out the menus and started on the shopping lists I should have done days ago. Fortunately, the specialty wholesaler I used for a lot of things was open on Saturday and would deliver by noon Monday—at the studio. I could pick up the rest of what I needed at Whole Foods or Trader Joe's on my way to the studio. I generally drove my car to our taping sessions, since getting to the studio on South State Street only meant a short distance on Lake Shore Drive and not a trip through the horrendous downtown traffic. As I would Monday, I often had lots to carry, but there was convenient parking and easy access.

Dusk came and went without my realizing it. I was so focused on my work that I barely heard Patrick's knock and didn't answer. He used his key and came cautiously in, peering around the partially open door and calling, "Henny? Why is it so dark in here?"

I looked around. The only light was my small desk lamp and my computer screen. The rest of the apartment was dark. "I'm working. Guess I lost track of time."

"I just wanted to check. Knew today was hard for you. You survive? Irene okay?" He flicked on the kitchen light.

"Yes and yes, but just barely." Suddenly I felt like crying. Whatever I'd been holding in all day bubbled to the surface, and silent tears ran down my face.

"Hey, didn't mean to make you cry."

"It's okay." Really it was more than that. Patrick was the only one in this whole mess who really cared about me. I wanted him to wrap me in his arms again, stroke my hair, and tell me he loved me. He just stood there, looking uncertain, while I inwardly railed against the gods for making him gay.

Trying to collect myself, I said, "I'm hungry. If you'll buy, I'll talk."

"Deal. Let me drop my stuff."

We splurged a little and went to Piccolo Mondo, one of Patrick's favorite places. Over a glass of wine, we shared an antipasto platter that had too much bell pepper for me. My entrée was whitefish, supposedly straight from the cold waters of Lake Superior, baked in a lemon, wine, and caper sauce. Patrick had the veal fixed almost the same way but with red peppers on it. He liked them. I didn't.

Once I began talking, everything spilled out—about the trust fund for Irene, her secrecy, the trip to the morgue, my second conversation that afternoon with John Wilson, the funeral that wasn't scheduled, even the bank statements. I ended with the fact that I was going to do my first solo taping Monday.

"You scared about the taping?"

"Yeah, I really am," I admitted.

He grinned. "Want me to come be your gofer? I can skip Monday, and I'm a pretty good hand in the kitchen."

For a moment I really wanted to take him up on it. But I knew that if I were going to manage the food segments on the *Today* show someday, I had to, as they say, put on my big-girl panties and do the tapings myself. After the first one, it would get easier. I was counting on that.

"Thanks. Yes and no, but I think I better do it myself. Irene might blow a gasket if she saw you on TV."

"Might shock her out of this catatonic state she seems to be in." He changed the subject. "Isn't it unethical for the lawyer to let you look at his client's bank statements?"

"Irene's his client now, so I guess as long as she agrees, it's okay."

"What exactly do you think you'll find?"

I pushed the last piece of fish around on my plate and thought about my answer. "I didn't tell Wilson this, but I hope I'll find out where Howard got his money." And that, indeed, was what was much on my mind. "And also whether or not he was bankrolling the show."

We shared tiramisu for dessert. There's a certain intimacy about sharing food, and I had to give myself a stern talking to. Afterward, we walked home. For late October, it was a pleasant night, still in the sixties with just a light breeze, though it was predicted to cool in the night.

"Supposed to be a gorgeous day tomorrow," Patrick said. "Want to rent bikes and ride out to the Point? Take a picnic."

"I have to work."

"You just told me you were pretty much all set. All you'll do tomorrow is fret and stew. Let's take your mind off it."

All of a sudden that sounded wonderful to me.

Chicago has a Bike Share program with rental stations all over the city. We rented ours from a station at Lake Shore and Fifty-Fifth and headed for the underpass to the Point. Promontory Point, part of the Burnham Park system, is a finger of land that juts out into the lake. It offers spectacular view of the beach at Fifty-Ninth Street and, from the north side, a sweeping view of downtown in the distance. We took a blanket, and the picnic I'd packed that morning using what I could find in the cupboard—tuna sandwiches, some brownies from the freezer, a couple of apples, and a bottle of chardonnay. I did put *Cooking with Irene* out of my mind, and I knew that day and that picnic would long stand out in my mind.

Chapter Fifteen

Monday, in my anxiety to get everything just right, I was at the studio well before our four o'clock for our afternoon shooting slot. I rushed in, carrying two bags of groceries Patrick and I had gotten from Trader Joe's the night before.

And there sat Irene, looking at her watch—the imperial Irene. "I would have thought you'd be here earlier. We tape at four."

I lapsed into my servitude. "Yes, Madame, I know that. I have everything ready. The grocery order should be in the refrigerator." I set down my bags to check the contents of the refrigerator. To my relief, everything was there.

She rose briskly, "What are we cooking this afternoon?"

I took a deep breath. "Hamburger Stroganoff with egg noodles, creamed spinach, and apple pie. And then Shrimp Victoria. They're for the cookbook."

"What? You expect me to make Stroganoff with ground meat? I have never done such a thing."

Was she trying for a Russian accent to fit the menu? "It's fairly easy and much more accessible for the audience of your cookbook.

Lots of households can't afford the beef tender that makes really good Stroganoff, and they don't want to cook a cheaper cut all day to tenderize it. Hamburger is the perfect compromise, and it tastes good."

She demanded the recipe, and I handed it over, reminding her that we would be shooting the actual paper copy she held. In other words, do not twist, tear, or bend. I did not ask what had changed her mind or why she was here, but I had my suspicions. She couldn't stand for anyone else to be in the limelight.

While I checked in groceries, laid out pots, pans, utensils, and ingredients, Irene studied the recipe. I would do the creamed spinach on the side, and the apple pie was—shhh!—from Trader Joe's. All Irene had to do was walk through the Stroganoff recipe, talking as she went. She would make it from scratch.

When push comes to shove, Irene can come through like a trouper, and she did. We shot the segment in almost one continuous take.

Next, we talked about the shrimp dish, which was basically shrimp sautéed in butter, sauced with sour cream, and served over rice. For color, I suggested we add a few capers, which also gave the dish a briny, acid balance for the rich sauce. Because it was an elegant dish, which she felt merited her skills, Irene approved it without change. The Shrimp Victoria was rich enough to be dear to her heart, and I made a note to use more sour cream in recipes.

The second session went equally well. I don't know if she'd been practicing or not, but she was fairly adept at one-handed cooking. Just enough of her left hand stuck out of the cast that she could use the fingers to steady a pot while she stirred with her right hand or pour ingredients into a pan. I didn't notice a tremor.

As we left, she took the rest of the recipes I'd worked on home with her to study. I was almost afraid to believe both the show and the cookbook would go smoothly.

Later, Irene did balk when I mentioned the tuna casserole for our next session, but I had to explain how it was updated. I think what convinced her was that I produced a bottle of French Sauvignon Blanc for use in the recipe.

* * *

Because I was now sort of ahead on recipes and planning, I was free on Monday to dive head-first into Howard's bank statements after Benjamin delivered them midmorning. Apparently, Howard did not abide by the conventional wisdom that you can discard financial documents after seven years. Another blessing was that he apparently didn't believe in shredders. I faced a wealth of material, if only I could pry loose its secrets.

Irene had swept up financial records indiscriminately and sent me a huge box of papers. The bank statements were easily identifiable, bundled by year and held together by rubber bands. I would begin there. My first decision was whether to begin at the beginning or with the most current statement and work my way back. I chose the earliest, which took me back to 1995, the year after he received his MBA.

The statements were from a downtown Chicago bank. His first monthly deposits were for $1,600, give or take a bit, but they were regular as clockwork, so I surmised he was working perhaps as an entry-level accountant for a CPA firm or some such. His expenses were minimal, apparently rent—that went to a corporation—and groceries. Oddly enough, he shopped at an A&P on Hyde Park Boulevard, sort of the northern edge of the neighborhood. Apartments line many streets at that end of Hyde Park, and I guessed he lived in a one-bedroom efficiency. The checks I identified as rent were for $450. Beyond that, Howard spent very little and apparently did not have a booming social life. He began, however, a lifelong habit that would account in part for his current financial position—whatever was left at the end of the month went into a savings account, and he started each month with a blank slate. Perhaps statements or an old-fashioned passbook for the savings account were among the other papers.

I stuck with the checking account statements. It was late Tuesday night, before I had a "Eureka!" moment. In 2000, everything changed dramatically. Huge expenses appeared on an American Express card I had not previously seen. I couldn't identify what they were without the American Express statements themselves, but I could guess. Foreign travel, especially since Howard's regular paychecks stopped in March.

It was late, and I was ready to stop for the night, but a question sent me back to my computer. When did Irene enter the picture? An online search for marriage records kept me up until nearly two in the morning, but I found it. They were married in a judge's office in Chicago in September of 2000. What happened between April, when he apparently stopped getting regular paychecks, and September?

The next morning we had an early taping. Ten o'clock, just one menu. I couldn't refrain from yawning, and Irene commented that I looked tired, and indeed I wasn't functioning at my best. I'm not one to get by on four or five hours of sleep.

"I know there is that young man living next door to you," she said. "Does he keep you up till all hours of the night?"

"No, Madame. I . . . I stayed up too late reading." Okay, it wasn't really a white lie. I did stay up reading—I just didn't mention that I was reading bank statements instead of a book.

We were planning to tape the tuna casserole, which didn't go well anyway. "I don't cook with canned fish. You will have to get fresh tuna, if we must use it."

"Madame, we are not grilling tuna steaks. We are making a casserole. It's like the Stroganoff—what your followers will have available to them. I got the very best albacore tuna in water at Trader Joe's. It's not like you're cooking with flaked bonito in vegetable oil." I was too weary to be diplomatic, but my words came back to bite me.

"Ugh, that Stroganoff dish. It was not fit to eat. I suppose this will be like that. I've heard of people using canned onion rings for a topping. Surely you aren't planning that."

"No, Madame. I will have buttered cracker crumbs ready for you to use. It will be good, I promise." But I knew she wouldn't admit to liking it, even if she did. But this taping too went well. We paired the casserole with a green salad with vinaigrette, French of course, and brownies I'd made from a mix.

I left on the early bus, anxious for a nap, her parting words ringing in my ears. "Get some rest, Henrietta. We cannot have an outstanding show if you are too fatigued to assist me."

"Yes, Madame."

It was a busy week. We had two more tapings scheduled for Thursday, and I was itching to get back to those bank statements. I considered cancelling the tapings—five was a lot in a week—but then I thought I should get them done while Madame was at least minimally cooperative. Then we could coast for a while.

* * *

I slept soundly for over two hours and then slapped together a BLT to eat at my desk, while I tried to figure things out. What did Howard do between April and September 2000? Where and how did he meet Irene? And where was Gabrielle that summer? I almost counted on my fingers until I realized Gabrielle was born in November 2000, so when they married, she was in Irene's belly. Howard married a hugely pregnant woman. Why? For love? And contrary to what Irene had apparently told her, Gabrielle was born in Chicago, not France. But that didn't tell me where she was conceived.

I found the key. Starting with the November bank statement Howard received a blind deposit of $10,000 each month—a whole lot of money back in 2000. His rent payments now went to The Dorchester Group, no doubt reflecting a move to a larger apartment. Dorchester was a main north/south street that intersected with Hyde Park Boulevard, where his A&P was. And he still shopped at the A&P, though grocery bills were larger now.

Was I truly doing valuable detective work, reconstructing the past, or was I building an imaginary structure in the air?

Patrick knocked when he came in from a late evening in one of his labs, but I assured him I'd already eaten, and I was really busy.

"You're no fun lately," he complained. "I thought you had all the menus planned."

"I'm trying to unravel the mystery of Howard."

He suddenly understood. "You're reading those bank statements, aren't you? What did you find?"

"If I tell you, will you go away and let me get back to it?"

"Yes, Mother, I'll go in my room and play with my toys."

I crumpled up a piece of paper and threw it at him. And then I told him about the missing summer.

"It all makes sense, Henny. I think you're on to something."
With a graceful but sarcastic bow, he was out the door, slamming
it behind him.

My mood was broken.

Chapter Sixteen

Thursday, I swore I was just going to confront Irene. What could she do? Fire me, for one thing, but I doubted it. I would begin with a question that occurred to me the night before. Who did she meet in the Loop the day someone pushed her off the curb? Was she sure she didn't see who it was? Then I'd just be bold and ask about her marriage to Howard—where did they meet? What happened in the summer of 2000? Maybe I could say that I loved a good romance, and I'd been so impressed by how much Howard loved her. It would be a little awkward, seeing as how I was not one given to girlish gushing.

I stiffened my spine, grabbed my backpack and the thermal bag that held our side dish, took the bus, and marched into the studio a little after ten.

Irene looked awful. Her mouth was drawn tight, her eyes wide with what looked like fright. She was pacing, clenching her hands, and when she saw me, she let out a sound that was half moan, half wail.

"I've been waiting for you. Something awful has happened."

Well, there went my questions. What awful thing could have happened? Howard was dead, so what could be more awful? Gabrielle? I stood stock-still and waited.

In her grief or whatever, Irene rushed toward me and grabbed my shoulders as though she would shake me. "Penny," she whispered hoarsely. She squeezed my shoulders tightly, and I resisted the urge to shake off her hands.

"What about Penny? I fired her, and you agreed. She can't hurt us."

She finally took a step backward. "That's just it," she said, "She can. She called late last night and demanded that we let her manage the cookbook project."

If that was all, Irene was really exaggerating. "I hope you said no way."

She shook her head. "I did. And then . . . that's when . . . she said, she said she can prove I killed Howard. And if we don't give her the cookbook job, she'll go to the police." The words came in a rush now.

"But you didn't kill him," I blurted out. "So what proof can she have?"

Irene was again drumming on the table where she sat, left hand still immobile in her lap. "But what if the police believe her?"

This was getting out of hand, and I decided it was up to me to calm her down. I was more interested in soothing Irene than I was in solving the problem of Penny. I spoke softly while trying gently to tell her she was foolish to believe Penny's threats. Honestly, I was afraid she'd fall off her chair because she was so upset. "Irene, she can't hurt you. The police will know her story is made up. I'll go to Detective Schmidt if I have to."

She shuddered. "That awful man!"

Just then the station manager, Ken, came ambling out of his office. Ken is a sort of laid-back guy, probably about Irene's age but the exact opposite in temperament. I'd seen more than once that he had little patience for Irene's drama. Now he ran a hand through his hair, cocked his head at her, and asked me, "She all right?"

"She's a bit upset," I admitted.

"Can you calm her down? We got to get going if you ladies are going to tape two shows this afternoon. What's the problem? Anything I can help with?"

"Uh, you might say it's a personnel problem. Someone who used to work for Irene has surfaced and threatened her."

His look turned to surprise. "Wouldn't be someone named Aldrich, would it? Called me a bit ago. I couldn't tell if it was a man or a woman—you know, deep voice. But I thought the first name was Penny."

"Yeah, it was and is. That would be her. She threatened to tell the police that Irene murdered Howard. She did *not* kill him."

"I thought he fell and hit his head! It really was murder?"

My big mouth. "Yes, it really was murder. But Irene did not do it. You haven't seen detectives around here after her, have you? What did Penny want from you?"

"Never figured it out. She blabbered on about a cookbook and it was her idea, but I couldn't figure out why she was telling me."

Irene had quieted enough to listen intently. "I'll sue her for . . . what do you call it? Slander."

I ignored her suggestion and said, "Irene. We've got to start taping."

"I don't know if I can." But she rose bravely and made for the restroom, saying she had to "fix herself."

Meantime, I unpacked the Potatoes Anna I'd brought from my home freezer. They were nicely thawed by now. I quickly stuck them in the oven, turned it on, and began laying out ingredients and utensils. Irene was gone long enough that I had time to do all the prep work I needed to—of course I'd done half of it at home the night before.

Taping did not go well. We were making meatloaf, which Irene disdained as peasant food, even as I told her to think of it as steak haché in a loaf pan. The potatoes, a French version of plain old scalloped potatoes, were my sop to her so-called aristocratic taste. I actually had made a meatloaf earlier in the week, froze it, and yesterday pulled it out to defrost in the fridge. I stuck it in the oven too. Irene would go through the motions of making it on camera and at the end, I'd produce the finished product and the potatoes.

Irene, however, couldn't do the hand-mixing of the meat, required if you were going to have a good meatloaf. Using a spoon, or heaven forbid, a hand mixer just didn't do it. And I knew she'd balk if asked to wear kitchen-type glove on her right hand. So I donned the gloves and did the mixing with a cheerful, "Let me help you, Madame." I was getting more comfortable on camera. She almost shoved me aside to thrust a large, wooden spoon into the mixture. I knew this would not result in an even texture. Then she dropped the spoon, and I had to dig for another. She spilled the broth we were using to bind the mixture and rebelled at coating the top of the meatloaf with seasoned tomato sauce.

I stopped the camera to explain that the finished meatloaf had a tomato topping and they had to match. Finally, she agreed, but it took us two hours to get thirty minutes of usable tape. We never did do a second show that day, but we were still ahead.

Irene had used Uber to get to and from the studio all week, Howard no longer being available. But she was always a little leery about the Uber driver, and this time she insisted I stay with her until the car arrived. That would have been okay, but she could not let go of the subject of Penny Aldrich, although I had dismissed it from my mind.

"Henrietta, you must do something about that Aldrich woman." Ignoring the first name was part of Irene's way of dismissing Penny as anything but a bother.

Do something? What? All I could think of was Archie Bunker telling Edith to "stifle." That's what I wanted to say to Irene. "I don't know what there is to do. She has no legal claim to the cookbook, and we have no obligation to her."

"The police," she hissed. "She'll go to that Detective Schmidt. She said she would."

"But what can she possibly tell him?"

She shook her head impatiently, as though I were slightly slow to understand. "Don't you see? She can lie. She can make something up, and they'll come after me."

I was as patient as I could be. "The police are usually pretty good at detecting a lie, especially if there is a revenge motive. She's got a grudge against you. They'll see that."

The head shake again. "We simply cannot count on it. You must stop her from going to the police."

Short of shooting her or some equally drastic measure, I could see no way to do that. Fortunately, the Uber arrived before I had to suggest that. And even more fortunate, the Uber driver was a middle-aged woman, the kind who looks like someone's mother. I had noticed before that Irene's assessment of people was often gender-based and almost amounts to all men are lustful, dishonest, and cruel, while all—or most—women were kind, caring, and trustworthy. I suppose today Penny Aldrich would be an exception to that generalization, but then Penny wasn't exactly a stereotypical example of femininity.

The driver identified herself and called Irene by name. She even got out and came around to open the back-seat door for Irene.

As she crawled into the car, I said softly, "Madame, I think you are expecting me to help you, but you are keeping secrets from me. I can't help you if you don't tell me everything you know."

She gave me a dark look and with a yank pulled the car door shut. The driver looked at me in surprise and then scooted back to the driver's seat without another word.

Driving home, I savored the thought of the weekend ahead of me. I wanted nothing more than to put Irene, Howard, murder, and cookbooks out of my mind. Maybe Patrick and I could picnic at the Point again or walk along the beach. A movie might be nice. I'd check the theaters when I got home . . . or maybe order Netflix. Then I had another thought: Patrick usually played basketball on Friday nights and came home, tired, dirty, and hungry, about eight o'clock. I'd fix dinner for him.

I ran over a list of possible dishes in my mind as I drove. The one that instinct told me was right was scallops in cream sauce. I'd find a basic recipe online and fiddle with it to see if I could make it my own—er, Irene's own—for the cookbook. For her, I'd call it Coquilles St. Jacques, the French name for the dish, and she'd love it.

I stopped at Whole Foods on the way home and got all the ingredients for the scallop dish and the mashed potatoes to go with it. We would have a rich dinner that night—lots of heavy cream.

To my surprise, Patrick's car was in its usual parking place when I drove up. Arms full of groceries, I struggled up to the third floor, and after I put the groceries down, I knocked on his door and called, "Surprise!"

He opened it slowly. "Henny, where've you been? Aren't you sort of late getting home?"

"That's my surprise. I stopped at Whole Foods. We're have Coquille St. Jacques for supper tonight."

"Who's we," he asked cautiously, "and what is that?"

"We is you and me, silly. Who else would I cook for? And it's a scallop dish in heavy cream sauce."

Patrick seemed ill at ease, looking down at his shoes and shuffling one foot nervously. Almost mumbling, he said, "Uh, Henny, I have a date tonight. Someone Maddie asked me to go out with."

Maddie! I knew that meddling cousin would be a problem. Well, at least she didn't know who he'd want to date. Instead of some hunky guy, I bet she'd found a sorority sister who would not steal his heart. Even so, I was a bit jealous. I wanted Patrick to myself, especially tonight.

I recovered nicely, or so I thought. "Oh, okay. Some other time."

"Can we eat the scallops tomorrow night?" He said it quickly, revealing his nervousness.

"Oh, you know fish and freshness and all that. I'll fix it tonight. Besides, it will take me a while. I have to fiddle with the recipe." I turned and went into my apartment, barely remembering not to slam the door in frustration.

I did make the scallops that night, but my heart wasn't in it. The only substitutions I made were chicken stock for clam juice and the omission of brandy because I didn't have any. I sliced mushrooms and diced shallots and worked away, deciding mashed potatoes would be too much trouble. I ended up putting a crumb topping on the dish rather than piping potatoes around it, and I did it as one large casserole and not the individuals that her recipe called for.

I had put the dish in the oven and begun cleaning up the kitchen when there was a soft knock on the door. Not Patrick's loud banging. Besides, I'd heard him go out, and I knew he wasn't home yet.

Maddie stood there expectantly when I opened the door. "Hi, there! I knew Patrick was out tonight, so I thought you might like some company. Even brought some wine." She flourished a bottle of chardonnay. I have a firm rule against drinking by myself, but that was the only reason I was glad to see her.

"Come on in," I said, hoping my voice wasn't as grudging as I felt. "Have you had supper?"

"No, honestly, I haven't. And something smells divine."

So while she chattered away, I cleared the table, poured two glasses of wine—it was chilled, so I knew she anticipated drinking it with me—and set the table for two. My mind was only half on her prattle until I heard her say, "My old roommate, Alison. I just thought she and Patrick would really hit it off. I hope they have a good time tonight."

Aha! So I was right. A sorority sister type. "Alison? Tell me about her." Not that I was at all interested. In fact, I was relieved.

"We went to Northwestern together. She's a lot of fun, and she likes sports, which should appeal to Patrick."

Guilt washed over me. Maybe I should have shown more interest in sports, especially his basketball games.

Dinner was divine, in spite of my uncertainty that night about my focus on cooking. I thought it one of my best efforts, and Maddie raved. "Whatever man gets you is one lucky guy," she said. "He'll never go hungry." There is was again, the reminder that Patrick and I were not a couple.

Chapter Seventeen

Patrick stuck his head in the door next morning while I sat nursing a cup of coffee and contemplating my day. The idea of a bike ride with him seemed to have vanished with the events of the night before. He confirmed there would be no bike ride, but for different reasons.

"Morning," he ventured.

I couldn't make my mouth behave. "Morning, Romeo. How was your date?"

"Oh, for Pete's sake, Henny." He came in and parked himself across the table from me. "Give me a break. Maddie arranged the whole thing. I know she meant well, but she just doesn't understand."

I almost giggled. He was right—Maddie didn't get it. "Well," I asked more seriously, "did you have a good time?"

"Alison was nice enough. We had supper at The Promontory . . . ."

I raised my eyebrows. The Promontory was more upscale than the places Patrick usually chose. Besides that it was a bit pricey, he just wasn't that much into chicken liver mousse and roast duck breast, though I would have liked to dine there. The one time I had, the menu intrigued me. I bit my tongue to keep from asking if Maddie had chosen the restaurant too. "What'd you have?"

"Fried chicken sandwich. Alison had some Brussels sprout appetizer and a small salad. I didn't even want to try that appetizer."

Of course he didn't. I wouldn't tell him how wrong I thought it was to order fried chicken in a place like The Promontory.

"And then we listened to a light jazz combo for a while, talked about nothing much. She likes sports so we did the Cubs vs. the White Sox thing. She wasn't much interested in basketball." He stood up. "I've got to be at school all day today—working on a project. But I'll be home late afternoon. Can we go for supper?"

I could have played it coy, but he knew perfectly well I had no other plans, and I knew that by the end of the day I'd want to quit working. "Sure. That would be nice."

After he left, I spent too long fiddling with recipes, avoiding that thick file of things from Irene. I did internet searches for recipes that we could adapt for Irene's cookbook. Found a few I thought she could live with—Rock Cornish game hens, stuffed pork chops, a quiche—aha, another French entry. I ruled out Lobster Thermidor on the grounds that lobster was too expensive but included another shrimp dish. And I thought we should have a sausage and kraut and beans menu. And enchiladas—maybe chicken enchiladas with sour cream sauce. Lots of ways to cook that. Somewhere toward noon I decided we now had about twenty recipes, with ten shows already taped. The cookbook was looking like a reality, and I was pleased with the progress we were making.

What, I wondered, really were Irene's favorites? I knew they would all be French, but I bet I could translate them. Then again, she'd want things like rabbit, which definitely did not appeal to most American cooks. And I was not going to mess up my Saturday by calling her.

After a light lunch of tuna salad, I picked up my exploration of Howard's papers. Going through bank statements is dull drudgery most of the time. I got so I was afraid I'd overlooked something important because I was bored and half-asleep. Then I'd have to go back and recheck a couple of months' worth of statements.

After a couple of hours, I made only one interesting discovery. Payments to The Dorchester Group stopped, and much larger payments began to an entity called Clarendon Realty. Each month, from March 2009 on, Howard wrote what appeared to be a rent payment. He transferred it from a second checking account that so far, I hadn't found. That March there was also a hefty check to a moving and storage company and two others that undoubtedly were furniture for the new apartment—one to Haverty's and one to Wayfair Furniture. Penny-pinching Howard had really splurged to get his family settled on the fashionable North Shore.

By three o'clock I was falling asleep over the 2014 statements and 2019 seemed a long way away. I slept soundly until five o'clock and then jumped out of bed as though I were late for something. Still foggy, I wandered around the apartment, turning on lights. When had it started to get dark so early?

Patrick and I went to Valois, a Hyde Park classic that I once heard was a favorite of the Obama family. It certainly was at the other end of the price scale from The Promontory. We walked to Fifty-Third Street, enjoying the crisp October air.

"Christmas will be here before you know it," I commented.

"Got your wish list made?"

"No. Not my shopping list either. Irene doesn't give me time. My mom will almost certainly insist I come home, but I don't know how to squeeze it in."

He sighed. "Yeah, I'll have to go home too."

Home for him was a lot closer than Texas. He'd only have to go to Skokie, and he'd probably see lots of Maddie during the holiday. I wondered if she'd trot Alison out for another try for the brass ring.

We both ordered catfish, fried crisp and good, and served with tartar sauce, which I thought an abomination and he liked. I went for lemon. With it we had turnip greens, something familiar to me but an acquired taste for Patrick. We didn't talk much as we ate, but on the way home he asked what I'd done all day.

I recounted the recipe search and the prowl through bank statements. "Only thing I found was the move to the North Shore in

2009. Howard must have felt pretty flush, because the rent went up a lot and he spent quite a bit on furniture."

"What about Irene's work? Was she contributing any income? When did she start the show?"

I twirled around and threw my arms around him, forgetting restraint and gayness and anything else. "You're a genius!"

Dumbfounded, he pulled away from me and looked around to see if people were staring. By then it was after eight, and we pretty much had Cornell Avenue to ourselves. "What're you talking about?"

"Wikipedia!" I said.

"Wikipedia? For what? All I know is that you can't cite it in scholarly papers."

"No. I have no idea when Irene started the show. I don't even know where she got her culinary training, if any. She won't talk about anything in her past beyond yesterday. Well, now beyond Howard's murder. But I'll tell her I need to do a Wikipedia entry on her. That will flatter her, and maybe she'll give me enough that I can begin to trace her life. There's got to be a clue to Howard's murder in there somewhere."

He shook his head. "Sounds like a long shot to me."

We walked a bit more, me savoring this new idea, although I had one disconcerting thought: would Irene lie to me? Fabricate a background that wasn't true. In a lot of ways, I didn't trust her.

Patrick wasn't done yet. "Have you heard from Gabrielle? She might be able to tell you some things. She was what? Nine when they moved to the North Shore? Surely she has memories."

"I've thought about calling her and put it off each time. I don't want to get roped into her search for her biolßogical father."

"Might be related to Howard's murder."

I stared at him. "You really are a genius. Of course it might be related. But I haven't a clue how to find out who he was or is."

"If you could find out where Howard was getting those monthly deposits, you might have the answer."

That was enough to make me resolve to hit the bank statements again in the morning.

* * *

Irene seemed to believe that you should start each week off with a serious Monday morning meeting. At least, that's the impression she gave when she called Sunday night and said imperiously that she'd expect me at ten the next morning. Sunday had been a long and fruitless day. I finished going through Howard's banks statements up to the present but had not learned one new thing. He was still in my eyes a frugal creature of habit. It would be a relief to do something else tomorrow, and then I laughed at myself. It was a cold day you know where when the long bus ride to the North Shore was my best alternative.

On that long bus ride, I had yet another chance to think about the tangle that was Irene and Howard's murder and Gabrielle's biological father, and my conscience pulled me to pay more attention to the present and quit trying to dig up Irene's past. So I was loaded with questions—two really—when I got to the Clarendon apartment.

Irene greeted me in a cordial yet businesslike fashion, and we were soon seated at the table, coffee poured but no croissants or other goodies in evidence. This clearly was to be a business session, though I wasn't sure what business she had in mind. I knew, however, what I had in mind, and I jumped in.

"Irene, before we talk about the show or the cookbook, it occurred to me I might be helpful to you in another way." (*That's called tact.*) "Have you made any arrangements for a service for Howard? I assume the funeral home has his remains"—what an awful term!—"but won't keep them forever?"

"Howard?" She looked blank for a second. Then, "Oh, he's here. He's in the bedroom."

For just a second there, I could picture Howard's corpse, fully dressed in one of his British-cut suits, lying on the bed. Ghoulish. I blurted out, "He is?"

Calmly she said, "Yes, he was cremated, and his ashes put into a special urn. I haven't decided what to do with them—I'm not sure I want them around, but then again it seems callous to simply discard them. I may scatter them someplace appropriate. Maybe Lake Michigan."

I hesitated. "Will there be . . . any kind of a service? You know, a memorial?"

"I don't think so. Neither Howard nor I had many friends. Oh, John Wilson would come, but that's about all. I didn't put an obituary notice in the *Sun-Times*, even though they called and tried to solicit one. Howard's gone, and that's that. Time to move on." She was almost brusque.

So poor Howard would go to his grave, so to speak, without much grief or attention. It gave me pause. But then I quickly moved on to my next topic. "Irene, how many of those little white pills do you have left?"

She shook her head and turned vague. "I don't know. Maybe a dozen. I'm not taking them."

"I know that, but you really should let me turn them in to a proper authority for you."

"Proper authority? Turn them in? I don't understand."

"They are an opioid. A highly addictive, dangerous drug called OxyContin. You shouldn't have them around the house if you're no longer using them. Around Gabrielle—or who knows? If an addict knew you had them, they might try to break in. I can turn them in at a licensed pharmacy."

She rose and began to walk around. "Break in? Is that why there was a *méchant* here just after Howard died?"

Oops. That one backfired on me. "No, Madame, I can't say that. I don't know. I just know that it's not a good thing to have them around. Why don't you go get them for me? I'll slip them in my purse."

She fixed me with a foxy stare. "How do I know you don't want to take them?"

"Madame!" I was truly so offended I was speechless.

Irene perhaps sensed she had gone a step too far and issued a highly artificial little laugh, not at all like her. "Ha, I was just joking." She sat down with a thump. "But no, I do not think I will give them to you. I may need one again sometime. What if *le tremblement* returns when this cast is off? Then I shall take a pill."

"Madame, the pill will do nothing for a tremor. Eventually those pills will expire."

"How long?" she demanded, and I was sorry I had said it.

"I don't know. I just know it is dangerous and wrong for you to keep them. I was only trying to help. Please consult your physician."

With a wave of her good arm, she dismissed that idea. "I do not trust him."

I didn't either if he'd given her a large prescription and not followed up, but now I guessed there was nothing for me to do but be watchful for signs that she had taken the medication.

Madame wanted to talk about the cookbook this morning, and once we got on that topic, she was full of enthusiasm. She wanted it what she called sideways—bound on the short side, a horizontal book—and she wanted plentiful color photographs. "We do not need that food photographer Penny spoke of. We can arrange food ourselves."

I wasn't sure about that. I wondered if Patrick had a good camera. Surely if he photographed the stars in the heavens, he could take credible pictures of food here on earth.

Irene had even saved samples of the typefaces she liked. Lots of script and italics, both of which would be difficult to read at any length. And she wanted an introduction, praising her cooking skills.

Aha! Better than Wikipedia. I was about to jump on that idea when her cell phone played an insistent version of *Le Marseilles*. She glanced at the caller ID and then held up a finger in my direction, as if asking me to hold on a minute, and muttered unhappily, "I must take this call." If I was disappointed that she didn't put the caller on speakerphone, I managed to hide it. In fact, I deliberately wandered into the kitchen in search of hot coffee. But not before I heard her say, in those distant tones of hers, "This is Irene Foxglove."

It was a short conversation, because when I came back from the kitchen, she had put the phone down on the table and sat with her hands in her lap. Her posture was rigid. "We cannot work anymore today. Detective Schmidt has commanded that I come to the police station. He is sending a car for me in an hour. Apparently, I have no choice in the matter."

Anxiety bubbled up inside me. "Do you want me to call John Wilson? You should have a lawyer with you."

"Pfft! He will do no good. I will defend myself."

What's the old saying about the man who is his own plumber has a fool for a plumber? Or maybe what I was thinking was, "Stupid is as stupid does."

"Do you want me to fix you something to eat before you go? It's almost lunchtime."

"No. I could not eat." Then, with a wicked grin in my direction, she said, "Perhaps I should take one of those pills."

I fell for it for a moment and said, "Oh, no, Madame."

She laughed heartily. I didn't join her.

I left the apartment before Schmidt's driver came, my notebook with scribbled notes on cookbook publishers, my mind burdened with worry about Irene. Because I'd left at an odd hour, I had to wait for the bus, but chilly as it was, I opted for a bench in Clarendon Park rather than sitting in the apartment and hoping Gabrielle didn't materialize.

Sitting there, I knew the first thing I must do: call John Wilson. Once again, he answered his own phone. When the story spilled out of me, all he said was, "I'll call Schmidt and direct him to wait until I get there. He subpoenaed Howard's bank accounts. That must be what prompted this. Mrs. Foxglove, uh Madame, is now not only a stubbornly independent woman, she is a very wealthy one." He assured me he'd be back in touch and ended the call.

Chapter Eighteen

Irene called that evening and in dramatic tones informed me that if she were incarcerated, I would have to take care of Gabrielle. My first wild thought was that idea surely gave me reason to pursue my search for Gabrielle's biological father.

Aloud, I said, "Irene, I truly doubt you will be incarcerated. And if you are, Gabrielle is nineteen and old enough to take care of herself. In fact, that's sort of what John Wilson hinted at. She gets only a modest gift from Howard's will. I bet he expected her to get a job."

"Gabrielle work? She has no skills."

And whose fault is that, I wanted to ask. "She can develop them. What is she interested in?"

"Clothes" was the brief and to-the-point answer.

"Then she could be a salesperson in a boutique."

"A shopgirl?"

I could imagine Irene recoiling in horror. Changing the subject, I asked how the questioning with Detective Schmidt had gone.

"Repetitive. He asked the same questions he asked before, but he asked them several times, each time changing the wording. I think he was watching for me to contradict myself. But I did not. I am innocent."

"Of course you are. What's next?"

"They're going to search the apartment, and that awful man wants to interrogate Gabrielle. I cannot allow that."

"You cannot stop it," I mimicked, though I worried about what Gabrielle would concoct in her twisted little mind.

She discontinued the call without warning, and I texted John Wilson to let him know I'd heard from her. He texted back that she was "difficult" in the interrogation, and he was nursing a comforting Scotch on the rocks.

I needed something comforting myself, because I was wondering why I was pursuing this as though my life and fortune depended on saving Irene, finding out who really killed Howard, and locating Gabrielle's father. In truth, none of that fell under the responsibilities of my job. I could continue work on the show and the cookbook as though none of this chaos swirled around me. Maybe a part of me was really selfish, scheming to protect her because if she were guilty the show would end and along with it my job.

But it wasn't just self-protection. Perhaps I was tilting at windmills, but I sensed an injustice, something wrong that had to be righted. If nothing else, the truth about the murder had to come out for Howard's sake. But beyond that, if I looked deep, I found that I was really fond of Irene. I saw beneath the façade to the insecure woman she was hiding. Somewhere, someone had hurt Irene badly, and she adopted her aloof French role as a shield. I suspected the person who hurt her was Gabrielle's father, but who was he and what did he have to do with Howard's murder?

Such thoughts made for a sleepless, restless night, and I finally fell into a deep sleep about four in the morning. Despite my resolve not to look at the clock every few minutes when I couldn't sleep, I peeked. I long ago found watching the clock when you can't sleep only makes it worse.

Irene called at seven—to tell me not to come to the apartment today. She was taking care of business. Foggily, I asked, "Are you leaving your apartment?" I remembered there would be a guard if she stayed there, but not if she went out into the world.

"I must," she replied crisply.

"What you must," I said, "is stay safe."

"I will be safe," she said.

I yawned. "Please call me when you return home." I may have been worried about her, but I couldn't babysit Irene every minute. I put the phone down and pulled the comforter back up around me, but sleep wouldn't come. Finally, about eight thirty, I got up, thinking coffee, some food, and a shower would perk me up. They didn't. Now I was sleepy and worried. Patrick was long since gone to school, and I couldn't call John Wilson every time Irene pulled a stunt. The thought of a lunch with Maddie crossed my mind, but I dismissed it. I wasn't in for fending off more questions about Patrick's social life—or lack thereof.

To cheer myself, I fixed my favorite breakfast—a runny poached egg on a piece of liberally buttered rye toast and some sliced sharp cheddar. Gooey and wonderful. I was just mopping up the last of the yolk with the tail end of my toast when Maddie knocked on the door. Taking a cue from Patrick, she didn't wait for me to invite her in, but just opened the door.

"You decent?" she asked.

Now that was a strange question. No, I wasn't eating breakfast in the buff, but what was her idea of decent? I doubted my baggy sweats with a matching, stretched-out shirt and my still-wet hair constituted decent. But, hey, I was in my own apartment and not expecting to go anywhere.

"I've found the most darling apartment," she bubbled. "I want you to come look at it with me." It registered on her, belatedly, that I was eating my breakfast. "When you're through, of course. May I pour myself some coffee?" And she did.

Striving for interest, I asked, "Where is it?"

"Kimbark, just south of Fifty-Sixth. In one of those gorgeous old houses. I guess it used to be the attic. "It's just perfect, and I can walk to class."

"Have you signed a lease?"

"No. I was waiting to show it to either you or Patrick. If you don't like it, I have a couple of others to look at."

I truly did not want to go apartment-hunting with her, but then again, I figured it would be better than sitting around worrying and feeling sorry for myself. I begged enough time to dry my hair and change into jeans and a sweater. Then I checked my phone, and we were off—in that red Jeep, of course.

It was as she said—charming. A lovely red brick, three-story house, tastefully decorated with traditional furniture. Sometimes, given the offbeat population at the university, you got ultra-contemporary furnishings, but this bordered on gracious living—wing chairs flanking a marble fireplace, a couch facing the fireplace, and a landscape painting hanging over it.

There were two flaws to this apartment that I could see. No private entrance—Maddie had to go through the house to climb the stairs to her hideaway. Once there, she had a living/bedroom combination and a kitchen but a shared bathroom. And you had to go into the public hall to go from one room to another, so if Maddie went from her living/bedroom to the kitchen or bathroom, she had to go out into the hall.

"The other person," she said brightly, "is an older schoolteacher. Very quiet."

I still didn't like the idea of a shared bathroom—where did you keep your toothbrush?—but I kept quiet. The main room was cute—two single beds, covered with blue and yellow plaid, doubled as couches during the day, and there was just enough room for a desk and bookcase. The kitchen was a Pullman-style space, so tiny I suspected it had once been a storage closet. Maddie seemed thrilled with the place, so I drummed up my enthusiasm, all the time blessing my roomy apartment over on Cornell.

Back in the car, she took another run at her Alison/Patrick dilemma. "Henny, are you dating anyone?"

"Not right now."

In a bold leap, she asked, "Are you interested in men?"

She seemed to have a knack for catching me off guard. I probably should have said something clever like, "Not really," and let her stew about it, but I was so taken back I blurted out, "Of course." Then I got more reasonable. "I just had a bad experience back home in Texas, and I'm not ready yet to play that game again."

All sympathy, she said, "Tell me about it."

And I found myself telling about the football hero, the wedding plans, the Austin apartment we'd found—and the big surprise two weeks before the wedding.

Maddie's reaction? "I don't suppose you're ready for lunch yet, are you?"

Here I bared my soul, and her mind was on food. "No, not really. And I do have some work to take care of."

So she dropped me off at the apartment, with a parting shot of, "I don't know how long Patrick will be patient. Have a good day."

How serious would it have been to throw a rock at her car? Maddie was sort of a puzzle. I didn't think she meant to be mean, she just sort of dithered into meanness innocently. And yet she couldn't be a dither head if she was going into a U. of C. fellowship. They just didn't take lightweights at that school. It was something I could never discuss with Patrick.

Once upstairs, I fixed myself a jug of iced tea and settled down to study cookbook publishers. It was twelve thirty, and no word from Irene was, I told myself, a good sign. At least there had been no ER calls.

The internet offers too many cookbook publishing opportunities. I had a long afternoon of research ahead of me. In college, researching for a term paper never intrigued me the way it does some. I preferred projects that were hands-on experiments. So sorting out publication possibilities for the cookbook became increasingly frustrating. I felt as if I were trying to unravel a tangle of yarn and had grasped an end, but if I let go for one second, I'd be back in a hopeless tangle again.

I'd paid enough attention in a marketing class I'd taken that I knew to disregard old-fashioned vanity presses. And I knew Amazon was an option, but I didn't know about several others, like Lulu or something called Cookbook Publishers. I made a chart on my legal pad—you might call it a manual database. But by doing that

I could sort out opportunities—some publishers offered design services, others didn't; prices varied wildly, as did the number of copies required. But one publisher wanted three hundred and fifty recipes! Another offered to make one sample copy for $39. *Irene's Favorite Forty* looked pretty slim in comparison. Another required two hundred copies, while by using something Amazon called Kindle Direct Publishing you could do print-to-order. After the initial setup, when you ordered one book or twenty, they printed them. But KDP had no design services, and I didn't know any designers. I suspected the wrong one could lead to disaster.

Madame would have firm ideas, I knew that, and I also knew her ideas, if unchecked, could also lead to disaster. I couldn't make an official decision, but I should be prepared to recommend and . . . persuade. But my head was swimming with endless variations of opportunities. I needed to talk to someone with more knowledge than I had, but who? I also needed some hard figures, not just ball-park guesses. With that in mind, I fired off a query to the firm that specialized in cookbooks. Pulling numbers out of the air, I asked for about five hundred copies of a two hundred-page book, with hard covers and color photographs. For the sake of specificity, I titled it *Irene's Favorite Forty and Other Recipes.*

Dusk was setting in when I looked up. Now that we were back on Central Standard Time, it got dark way too early for me, and by five the world outside my windows was turning to gray. It took me a minute to realize that I hadn't yet heard from Irene. Was she safely home? Should I start worrying? What if I called to check on her and caught her in an embarrassing moment—though I couldn't think what that could be.

Chapter Nineteen

I was still thinking, a bit more worried now, when Gabrielle called. "Where's my mother?" she demanded without so much as a hello.

"I was just wondering that myself. Do you know where she went? What time did she leave?"

Gabrielle considered these questions trivial or demeaning or something, because her answer was abrupt. "She was gone when I got up"—that could have been noon for all I knew—"and I have no idea where she went, don't care. I'm hungry. And she's not answering her cell phone."

Ah! We got to the point behind the call. "Fix yourself something to eat. Scramble a couple of eggs, make a cheese sandwich, see what leftovers you have in the refrigerator."

"I don't eat leftovers, and I don't know how to cook."

Did her tone really imply that I should rush right up to the North Shore to feed her, or was I being hypersensitive? "Well, then, call for a deli delivery. Howard apparently had a deli he used frequently."

"I have no money, and they won't let you run a tab."

And you're too old to be so helpless! Maybe Howard had left an unpaid bill at the deli, but surely this spoiled brat could figure out some way to feed herself. Gnaw on a crust of bread if nothing else. I was disgusted. "Gabrielle, you'll have to take care of yourself. Please remind your mother to call me when she comes in." I hit end before she could sputter in indignation.

But now I was worried, the kind of impotent worry that comes because you can do nothing about whatever is going on. I tried the cell phone myself and got no answer, so Gabrielle had been right about that. My imagination worked tirelessly, but the scenario I kept coming up with was that she had been attacked again, this time with more serious results than a broken arm. She was lying in an ER, unconscious, with a concussion. But surely someone would have gone through her purse, found some ID, and called Gabrielle. Or maybe the person who attacked her had stolen her purse.

Patrick wasn't home, and I couldn't call John Wilson every time Irene did something flaky or dangerous. But still, I was writing an entire mystery novel in my head. The ring of my phone put a temporary end to my imaginings.

"I'm safely home," Irene said crisply. "You must not worry about me, because I cannot report to you every minute."

Arrogance, or at least a lack of gratitude, ran in the family. "I hope you'll feed Gabrielle," I said. Okay, I admit that was a touch of nastiness.

"She is about to learn to make an omelet." Her tone was still brusque.

"Good luck," I said aloud, while thinking how like Irene it was to start Gabrielle with one of the cooking skills hardest to master. I remembered hearing Jacques Pépin—I think that's who it was—say that if you ever wanted to check out a chef's skills, ask him or her to make an omelet.

Irene's voice broke into my musing. "I'll see you in the morning. Try to be here at ten sharp."

"Yes, Madame." She wouldn't recognize sarcasm.

One more interesting phone call awaited me that night, though I didn't know it when I followed my advice to Gabrielle and started exploring my refrigerator. Looked like it was tuna for me—I'd make one of those open-faced tuna sandwiches on a crispy baguette. Olive oil instead of mayonnaise, and anchovies and capers for flavor. I had just pulled out an egg and set it to boil when my phone rang insistently.

The caller's number was not familiar, and I was about to ignore the call when I realized the name Schmidt meant the North Side detective was calling, and it had to be about Irene.

"This is Henrietta James," I said in my most formal tones.

"Ms. James, I need some help. That is, if you've got any insight."

Insight into what? If he meant Irene, I could write a book for him. "I'll try."

"Did you know that Mrs. Foxglove left her apartment today and was gone most of the day?"

"Yes, I did know that, but she's safely home now. She called me just a few minutes ago."

"Do you know where she went?"

"No, sir."

He let out an expletive and then apologized. "This case is going to drive me crazy. She went downtown, took an Uber, and had lunch at the Palmer House, met an unidentified man there. Do you know who that could be?"

I went from wondering how he knew this to the quick realization that he'd had her followed. "I thought you said you couldn't protect her if she left the apartment."

"I wasn't protecting. I was, I wished, detecting. I had a tail on her to see if her movements would tell us anything. She and that man lingered a long time over lunch, but it wasn't a casual happy affair. My guy tells me they seemed to be arguing. Lots of hand gestures, raised voices. But here's the kicker. They talked in French, so even at the next table, he couldn't tell what they were saying." He sighed in exasperation. "Who knew I should have cops who speak French?"

I couldn't help but grin. "Typical Madame," I said. "So did you find out who the man was?"

A disgusted negative sound. "Nope. They parted, and my tail had to decide which one to follow. The order was to tail her, so he did."

"She just got home a bit ago," I repeated. No need to tell him about Gabrielle's pitiful call. "So where else did she go?"

"That's what has me worried. She went to a gun shop."

I gasped. "I never would have thought Irene would buy a gun."

"At first she didn't. She came out of the shop empty-handed, presumably because she didn't have the identification card gun owners are required to have, and there's a twenty-four-hour wait to get one, so she couldn't legally buy one today. But she didn't give up. Your chef is one determined lady. She went to three different gun shops and apparently got turned down. She finally had her Uber take her to a pawn shop on the West Side. And she scored."

I was glad he couldn't see me, mouth open, head shaking in disbelief. "Irene doesn't know a thing about guns. Howard hated them."

"Well, I hope she got a lesson, because she's got one now. And she's cost some pawnbroker a lot of money. We'll have to fine him and close him down for a period of time. Selling a handgun illegally is a felony in Chicago."

"Can't you just take it away from her?"

"Wait," he said abruptly, "there's more. She next went to Lincoln Park and sat on a bench." He paused, apparently for effect. "For two hours."

"Two hours? What did she do?"

"Nothing. Just sat there, staring at the lake. My guy was afraid she was going to use the gun on herself, so he hid close by and watched. And kept checking his watch. Finally, she gets up and walks to a parking area where a car is waiting. Seemed to be the same Uber she'd been using all day."

"So now she has a handgun." It was a statement, not a question.

"We'll have to confiscate it, of course. And charge her with illegal possession. My question to you—oh, damn, I have so many. Is she a danger to herself? To someone else?"

My answer was slow as I thought through his questions. "Irene would never hurt herself. I'm positive about that. And of course she'd never hurt Gabrielle. She knows now she's in danger, and I suppose she wanted the gun for self-protection. Or maybe she'll go after whoever she had lunch with. If she knows where to find him. I don't think she does. She may know how to contact him, or he may set up their meetings."

"Meetings plural?"

I told him about the errand in the Loop the day she broke her arm. "The mysterious man was almost certainly who she met, and I thought he probably pushed her off the curb."

Schmidt had apparently reached the end of his rope for the evening. "I give up. I'll go see her tomorrow. You be there?"

"Ten o'clock," I said, "or a bit after."

"Okay. Keep your ears and eyes open. I need all the help I can get on this one."

With the call ended, I thought to myself, "Now I know another reason I'm so determined to get to the bottom of all this—who killed Howard, who is Gabrielle's father. It's because John Wilson and Detective Schmidt think I can figure Irene out, when they can't."

My sandwich tasted like sawdust, and Patrick hadn't yet come home when I went to bed, so I had no one to pour out my troubles to. Maybe Mom was right, and I should broaden my social circle.

* * *

Next morning, Detective Schmidt was sitting in a parked car outside the Foxglove apartment building. When he saw me, he got out and walked in with me. I was pretty certain that was not a good move, but I didn't say anything. Irene did, however, when she opened the apartment door.

"Why did you bring him?" It was not exactly a welcome.

"Coincidence," I muttered and tried to slip by her.

Detective Schmidt was not intimidated. Standing in the doorway, because Irene physically blocked any further entrance, he said, "Mrs. Foxglove, I need you to give me the handgun you bought yesterday."

She sputtered. "That's ridiculous. I have no idea what you're talking about. Gun? I would never buy a gun."

"May I come in? I don't think you want to air this for your neighbors." With a gentle hand on her arm, he pushed here aside and entered the apartment, closing the door behind him.

Irene was visibly agitated, clutching her left arm with its cast in her right hand and shaking with anger. "You can't come in here without a search warrant. I know my rights."

Schmidt remained calm. "Mrs. Foxglove, I'd advise you to cooperate. One of my men tailed you to the pawn shop yesterday and saw you purchase the gun. I could easily arrest you and charge you with at least a misdemeanor. If I wanted to be truly hard, I could push it up to a felony. But I'm not doing that. I'm just asking you to give me the gun."

I found my voice. "Irene, you best do as he says."

"You keep your opinions to yourself." She whirled to face me, her face distorted with anger—or guilt.

In the background I heard a stifled laugh. Turning I saw Gabrielle disappear back into the kitchen. Irene had switched her glare from me to the vanishing figure, and I could feel the tension in the air. Schmidt remained determined and not at all flustered.

"The gun, Mrs. Foxglove."

It occurred to me that Irene might be doubly embarrassed to have this take place in front of me. It could, in her mind, undo whatever authority or superiority she had. "Irene, would you prefer that I come back another day?"

For a minute, she looked startled out of her anger, as though she had just come back to reality. "No, no. We must work. You wait in the sunroom."

The woman had never heard of the word, "Please." I wandered off to the sunroom and settled in one of the overstuffed chairs, looking for something to read. A copy of *Food & Wine* lay on the side table, and I leafed through it. The recipes were all too full of fusion Asian to interest me, given that my push these days was on America's rich blending of cultures to create our own cuisine. Behind me I heard low, muffled voices.

At long last, I heard a door close. Expecting to be called, I laid the magazine aside. But instead Irene apparently made a phone call. I could hear a one-sided conversation but no matter how I strained—and I did!—I could not make out the words. Finally, I heard a drop in her voice that sounded like she was ending the conversation. And then she called out.

"Henrietta, come! We must get to work. We have wasted valuable time with this foolishness."

I guess that was one way to look at it.

When we were seated at the table, she said, "John Wilson will be arriving a little after noon. He's bringing lunch when he comes to discuss this matter of the gun and what I must do next." She shook her head, indicating impatience with the entire business. "What do you have for me today?"

Talk about role reversal. She had completely given up the responsibility for the show and the cookbook, and now it all fell to me. It was as though I had become Howard. Fleetingly I thought of asking for a raise, but I dismissed the thought as poor—and unkind—at this time.

"Madame, let's begin with the cookbook." I laid out three alternatives as clearly as I could. I'd even made a copy of my cheat sheet for her to study, but she barely glanced at it and then said, "You decide."

I took a deep breath and told her, "I've asked for costs on a two-hundred-page book with hard covers and color photographs."

That got her attention. "Whatever would I say for two hundred pages? How many recipes is that?"

"I don't know exactly, but much of the book will be taken up with other things—an introduction, a biography of you, an index, and pictures—lots of pictures. We can not only film the finished dish, but we can have shots of you preparing it, illustrating the steps."

"How many recipes?" she repeated.

"We can have a section of menus, for *Irene's Favorite Forty*, as we discussed, and then we can do sections for entrees, salads, soups, desserts—and each section would have an introductory page. It's not as impossible as it seems now when it's almost all a blank slate." I ignored her question and plunged ahead.

She was stuck on how many recipes and repeated wonderingly, "Two hundred pages."

"Madame, to attract readers we will want to have a short biography of you, emphasizing of course your French background." Flattery will get you almost anywhere, I thought.

"Of course. You write it," she said.

"I need a little background." Pen poised over my legal pad, I asked, "Where were you born?"

"That doesn't matter," she said.

"We need to be truthful with our readers. Tell me where."

Reluctantly, "Minnesota." And then having loosened a memory, more came out. "Irene Lindberg. From that poor Lindberg family, where the mother died too young. I was ten, and I had two younger sisters and a brother. I became the cook. Our father was a dairy farmer, but not a successful one." She looked at me. "Don't say all that."

"How about if I say, 'Born in the Midwest'? School?"

"I went to a small-town school. Goodhue, Minnesota. It was bigger when I was young than it is now. There was no money to send us girls to school. My father sent my brother. He's a wealthy physician now. My sisters married farmers and raised babies." There was a touch of bitterness in her tone. "I went to work as a shopgirl in St. Paul, rented a room in a boardinghouse. The woman who owned it was a good cook and took me under her wing, taught me some basic skills that my own mother had not lived long enough to show me. Mostly she taught me the things I'd been doing wrong."

Fascinated that she was finally revealing so much about herself, I asked if the boardinghouse food had an influence on her cooking. That got me a slight smile, just the barest curve of the lips.

"Yes. It taught me to avoid heavy, starchy meals with lots of potatoes and shy on the meat."

Moving right on, I asked how she got to Paris. "I sold lingerie in a small shop, me who had nothing but raw cotton underwear all my life. The owner saw my fascination with good clothes and told me about opportunities for young women abroad, taking care of rich people's children. Lord knows I knew enough about taking care of younger children by then. I went through an agency and became an au pair."

"Who was your host family?"

She waved a dismissive hand in the air. "There were several. It doesn't matter. We can't identify them in the cookbook."

I should have pushed for identities, and I knew it. But I also knew she could both clam up on me or outright lie, and neither of those would get me anywhere. I took a different tack. "Did you learn to cook with these families, or did you take formal training?"

Drawing herself up straight with pride, she replied, "I studied at Le Cordon Bleu."

I thought she really believed it herself, but I still thought she probably went to the Kendall Cooking School right here in Chicago. With Irene in such a cooperative mood, we worked right up until the moment John Wilson arrived, bringing croissant sandwiches and sides of Caesar salad.

After greetings, I excused myself, saying I knew they didn't need me for their discussion, and I had to write up my notes. At John's urging, I took my lunch with me to eat at my apartment.

Irene was all smiles as she reminded me, "We tape tomorrow at seven in the evening. It will be a long evening, so get plenty of sleep."

I had no idea during that long bus ride what surprise awaited me at home.

Chapter Twenty

At first, I was pleased with the rapid response from the cookbook publisher. He wrote: "Ms. James, we are pleased to have your query and will be happy to provide you with an estimate and work with you, should you so choose. However, I am a bit puzzled. Just yesterday, I received a proposal, followed by a strange phone call, for a cookbook so similar to what you propose that the titles echo each other. This was *Forty Favorites from Ina Faye Clark*."

I almost threw my coffee cup across the room in anger, but fortunately such drama was not really me. However, I did have to pace around my kitchen before I read further.

"I am not a believer in coincidence, so I would like to understand what's going on here. If you would care to talk about it, you can call me. I will leave instructions your call is to be put straight through to me."

It was signed Rob Pierce, publisher.

Sitting in stunned disbelief for several minutes, I finally got myself together, checked my watch, and dialed. It was two thirty in Chicago, so whatever part of the country Mr. Pierce was in, he was undoubtedly in his office. The receptionist who answered said, "Rob's expecting your call. Let me ring him for you." I liked the informality I sensed when she called her boss by his first name, but I still expected an older man. Somehow my mind conjured up a picture of a small, stooped man, balding, with a green eyeshade and a stub of a pencil clutched in his fist. Bartleby the Scrivener come to life.

Rob Pierce did not sound at all like Bartleby. His voice was firm, with a hint of laughter, and he took over the conversation immediately. "Thanks for calling. I really want to get to the bottom of this. We can't have conflicting projects inhouse, and I suspect there's a story behind this seeming coincidence."

"Mr. Pierce, was the proposal submitted by a woman named Penny Aldrich?"

A short laugh was followed by "Yes. You know her?"

"Unfortunately, I do. She was publicist for Irene Foxglove, the Chicago TV chef, until I fired her."

"And you are?"

"Ms. Foxglove's assistant. It's a long, tangled story."

"I'm all ears."

As briefly as I could I explained about Howard's murder and Irene's seeming inability to take over, which had forced me to make some decisions. I did not go further into such bizarre things as the handgun, but I did elaborate on the history of Penny, Ina Faye, and Irene. When I paused for breath, he let out a long, low whistle.

"Wow, quite a tangled story. I'll be quite frank with you. Ms. Aldrich rubbed me the wrong way. Too pushy. Too determined we had to sign on the dotted line right away. I'm new to this business. Inherited it from my father-in-law, and as the new kid on the block, I'm cautious. I had a gut feeling about this one."

"Mr. Pierce, what did you tell her?

"Call me Rob. I just stalled. Now I'm glad I did. I'd like to work with you. I have a few questions and a piece of advice."

"Okay."

His questions had mostly to do with content and the nature and audience for the book. When he heard my explanation about it being time to focus on American cooking and its blend of cultures, he liked it and made some good suggestions. His advice?

"Cobble together a manuscript, even if it's twenty pages—something concrete with a title page, dedication, and acknowledgments. Include a statement that all recipes are original to your chef—they are, aren't they?"

I nodded as if we were Facetiming, which I was a bit sorry we weren't. I wanted to see what he looked like. Wondered if he looked as good as he sounded.

"After the title page, put a page with the statement, 'Copyright Irene Foxglove' and insert the copyright symbol. Make three copies of this—put one in a sealed envelope and mail it to yourself; mail one to me; and keep one for your working copy."

If he was new to this, he'd apparently learned fast. "Why am I mailing one to myself?"

"I'm not sure this would hold up in court, but we generally advise clients to leave an envelope containing the copy unopened someplace safe, a deposit box if they have one. It will indicate the date you filed for copyright, because the envelope will be postmarked with a date."

Scribbling furiously as he talked, I made a note to give the envelope to Patrick, since I didn't have a safe deposit box. I don't know if I thought Penny would break into my apartment and steal it or what, but I knew it would be safe with him.

"Thanks. You've given me plenty to work on," I said.

"Good. I'll get right on the estimate when I get this from you."

We hung up, and I sat balancing anger against enthusiasm. My anger at Penny's continual betrayal was pretty intense for me, and I longed for some kind of retribution. But I figured edging her out on the cookbook was enough. My enthusiasm for working with Rob Pierce was at high tide, and I wondered if it was solely for the project or maybe Mr. Pierce himself had something to do with it. Instinctively I knew Patrick would be hurt if he thought that.

Speak of the devil. Patrick came home early and stuck his head in to say he had to go back to work that night. "But I got to catch up," he said. "What's the latest with Irene?"

"How long do you have?"

He seriously looked at his watch and said, "Oh, thirty minutes at least."

"Come on in, and I'll tell you all."

Patrick settled on the couch, and I stayed perched at my computer, turning my chair to face him. Where to begin? The handgun seemed most important to me, so I told that story first, and he responded with proper surprise.

"Irene with a handgun? I don't know this lady, except what you tell me, but that seems an unlikely combination. And not a good one."

"That's what Detective Schmidt thought. He confiscated the gun. But I did get a start on getting some background on Irene. Born in Minnesota. Irene Lindberg, from a poor farm family. Mom died young, and she had to take over."

He shook his head. "No France?"

"Oh, she was there. As an au pair, but I can't verify it."

"You need to lean on her to find out who and where. I'm suspicious."

"So am I," I assured him.

We talked about schedules. He had to go back to his lab or telescope or whatever but was looking forward to a long weekend. I told him we were taping at seven tomorrow, Friday.

"Seven at night? And then you'll come home from that neighborhood alone at what time of night? Eleven? Twelve?"

"Ten, if I'm lucky."

He stood up decisively. "I'm going with you. It's time I met the fabled Irene, and I don't like you alone at night in what is virtually inner city." After a pause in which he apparently had another thought, he asked, "What about Irene? How does she get home?"

"Uber."

"We'll wait to see her safely with her driver."

I loved the way he was taking charge and being so protective—or did I? "I usually do," I said.

Patrick went off to do his thing, and I threw myself into putting together what Rob Pierce had called front matter, including a carefully worded bio of the chef.

* * *

Friday evening Patrick knocked on my door about six thirty. He was all spiffed up—crisp jeans, an Oxford cloth shirt, and a blue Patagonia jacket that made his eyes pop. I managed to stop myself from swooning and handed him bags of groceries. Grabbing my computer backpack, I followed him downstairs to his car. He was being gentlemanly and insisting on driving, though I kept assuring him I knew where we were going better than he.

We got to the studio a little before seven and found it empty, so that I could begin setting up. Irene blew in about seven ten, apparently in a cheerful mood. Spotting Patrick, she said, "And is this the young man who keeps you up too late at night?"

Patrick deadpanned it. "No, ma'am. It's the other way around. She keeps me up." Then with a grin, he held out his hand. "Patrick O'Malley. I'm pleased to meet you."

Leaning in close to him, she said, "You naughty boy. I'm sure you keep Henrietta from her work."

I was thinking if she kissed his cheek, I'd deck her. Aloud I said, "Irene, we're almost ready. Best get your apron on. If we can do this in one take, we can all be out of here at a decent hour." In truth, I was thinking of my stomach. We hadn't had supper before we left, and lunch seemed long ago and far away.

We were doing a spring lamb stew this night. Don't ask about finding spring lamb in the market in November. I was fearful it would be mutton, but I did the best I could, chose the smallest leg available before asking the butcher to cube it.

Irene protested the stew at first, naturally. She wanted to do a French gibelotte, a stew usually made with rabbit. I assured her that few American cooks had the fortitude to cook rabbit. She was appropriately horrified and muttered something about that barbaric part of the country from which I came. As it was, her recipe was pretty much Julia Child's, but I didn't worry about plagiarism—there's only so much variation you can work in stew. And Irene would give it her own twist in her patter as she talked.

She was still awkward, cooking with one useful arm, and I made a mental note to ask Monday how long she'd have the cast. But she had gotten better at this one-armed cooking and didn't spill or drop anything, making my job much easier. I supplied her with pre-measured amounts of flour, salt, and pepper to coat the meat, garlic, beef stock, red wine, and various herbs. Frozen vegetables work fine in stew when not in season, so we had peas and carrots, tiny new potatoes (scrubbed but with the skins on), and frozen pearl onions. I don't mind stripping a piece of potato skin off to let it expand with cooking, but I draw the line at peeling all those tiny onions.

Since stew must simmer either stove-top or oven for hours, I had brought a finished pot for the final shot. After Irene took a spoon to dip in and taste the broth, she motioned to Patrick, who had been sitting quietly watching.

"Come here, you wonderful young man. Taste this and tell us what it needs."

I was appalled. He was going to be on camera, but there was nothing I could do about it at this point. The cameras were rolling. Patrick obediently walked over to stand next to her, and she held out her hand to me for yet another clean spoon. Then, simultaneously, they each tasted it, and she stared intently into his face. It was outrageously flirtatious.

"Well?"

Patrick was good, I had to give him that. "More salt," he said.

She seemed about to deflate like a balloon, but she quickly brightened and turned toward the camera. "Isn't he great? I'm going to have him taste all my dishes. And that, *mes amis*, is how you make lamb stew. Simple, no? And delicious."

Ken called it a wrap just before she could dip her spoon back into the stew. No double-dipping allowed on camera.

Irene was all over Patrick, claiming he must come back often and scolding him for keeping me up late. I knew her mind was envisioning mad passionate nights on Cornell Avenue, but I saw no tactful way of correcting her. She requested her Uber, and we waited inside for the driver since it had gotten chilly.

When the car came, we confirmed the driver's identity and he confirmed that he was picking up Irene Foxglove to go to an apartment on North Clarendon. Patrick helped her into the back seat and then walked around to talk to the driver. Unobtrusively, he tipped the man. After the driver took off, Patrick told me, "I asked him to be sure to see that she got safely into the building."

"Good. I don't suppose Schmidt still has his protection in place."

At first, on the way home, Patrick was so silent that I was bursting to know what he was thinking. What was his impression of Irene?

Finally, he spoke. "She's something else, isn't she? I know that was an act put on for me, but why did she do it?"

The only answer I could come up with was, "To boost her own ego."

"Seems almost manic-depressive, not that I'm any authority. But you've described her down moods, feeling sorry for herself, unable to take command. And yet she was none of that tonight. Clearly on a high."

Oh good, he'd given me something else to worry about, but I guessed I had worried about Irene's mental stability all along.

We went back to my apartment. I had brought the premade stew back home with me, leaving the one into which Irene double-dipped for the clean-up crew. I heated steaming bowls in the microwave, which Irene would see as a sacrilege, but it was nearing ten o'clock, and we didn't want to wait for the whole pot to heat. I'd have good leftovers for the weekend.

It was late when Patrick left for his own apartment, and I was sleepy. Turning to say goodbye, he said, "I have something to do in the morning, but let's count on supper tomorrow night. Okay?"

I nodded and, naturally, asked, "What are you doing in the morning?"

He smiled like a cat. "Secret," he said, as he pulled the door closed behind him.

Chapter Twenty-One

Next morning I heard Patrick leave about ten o'clock. Within an hour, he was noisily back, making two trips up and down the stairs. Each time his footsteps indicated he was carrying something heavy. Thereafter, I heard hammering and various sounds of metal on metal. Curiosity ate at me, but I was too proud to go find out what he was doing, so I tried to busy myself with that darn cookbook. How many ways can you say she wasn't really born in France, but she identifies as French?

Finally, about noon, Patrick stuck his head in my door and said, "Come look at what I got this morning."

Feigning reluctance, I got up slowly and followed him, but all my pretense disappeared when he threw open the door to his apartment. A gleaming black barbecue grill dominated the middle of his living room, complete with a gas tank, a couple of shelves for warming, and a side work tray.

"It's wonderful!" I said. Of course, I should have stopped there, but I didn't. "You can't grill in the middle of your living room."

He rolled his eyes. "I don't intend to. This beauty goes on my back stoop."

In Texas, we don't have stoops; we have porches. So I questioned him. "Stoop?"

"Of course, the back porch."

Patrick's apartment was what I assumed was the back half of a once much-larger unit, while mine was the front half. That would explain why his living area was at the very rear, the largest room which had originally been a kitchen, while mine was at the front— once the living room. Like mine, his living area and kitchen were together. Our bedrooms were sort of adjacent, with the apartment walls between them. So, yes, he had a back porch. I'd just never looked at it. In truth, I'd not spent much time in his apartment, since we always seemed to hang out in mine.

"Come on," he said, picking up one end of the grill. It rolled easily, and he led the way out to this stoop. It was small, as to be expected, but big enough for the grill and two chairs.

"So what's for dinner tonight?" he asked.

"Are you going to grill?"

"Of course, milady. But first we must shop and decide what we want."

At Whole Foods, we studied the meat counter, then wandered over to the fresh seafood, and then back to the beef, torn between steak and grilled salmon. We finally decided on the salmon and then proceeded to the vegetable section, where we chose roma tomatoes, a sweet onion to quarter, a zucchini, and a few mushrooms. Patrick had gotten a vegetable basket, so we would have grilled vegetables and baked potatoes. I nixed the bell pepper but agreed to do twice-baked potatoes and a butter/anchovy sauce for the salmon.

Patrick nearly dragged me to the pastries. "No, we're not going to grill dessert . . . " He looked like inspiration hit. "We could grill fruit. No, we'll have a decadent dessert."

We settled on a chocolate eclair for him and a mini chocolate mousse for me. Laden with groceries, we headed home.

As he put the sack with my groceries on the table, Patrick warned, "I expect company while I'm grilling, but it will be cold. Be sure to wear a jacket. See you about seven."

You'd have thought I had a big dinner date, I took such care with dressing. I wanted to be just right, yet casual. Jeans, yes, but what on top? Eventually I decided on an après ski sweater, bearing in mind what Patrick had said about cold. It was a lovely blue with a sort of Norwegian pattern at the neck, and I always felt comfortable in it. My only concern was that I'd be too warm while we ate inside—surely, we would not eat on that little stoop. Off came the après ski top and on went an oversize white linen shirt over a blue turtleneck. As I put on light makeup, a horrible thought occurred— what if he had also invited Maddie? Surely not. We only bought enough salmon for two.

Promptly at seven I was in his living room wearing my ski jacket and carrying the potatoes. Patrick had turned on the grill already, so he whisked the potatoes over to keep warm on one of the extra shelves. Then he poured wine, and glass in hand I followed him to the stoop. The vegetables smelled heavenly—he had brushed them with a homemade vinaigrette—and the salmon went on the grill, which he had carefully greased so the fish would not stick.

Sitting, watching him grill, I was silent, taking in the whole scene. He was obviously at ease working with food, and I'd been making a mistake not to let him do more, even in my kitchen. Although her approach was totally wrong, maybe Irene was more insightful about Patrick and food than I was.

My thoughts wandered to the marriage I'd thought I'd have. This was just the kind of scene I'd dreamt of with the jock who didn't know squat about cooking. I'd been fooling myself about a lot of things.

Patrick carried the food inside, and we ate at the table that doubled as a kitchen table and a desk. I hadn't noticed when I came in, but he'd set it with linen placemats and a single candle. Glasses of ice water sat at each place. I did feel like I was on a date.

Dinner was delicious, and we concentrated on enjoying the food. Patrick offered coffee, but I declined in favor of a second glass of wine with my mousse. White wine with chocolate is one of earth's great delights to me. We lingered, me licking the chocolate off my fingers, and him laughing because I had it on my chin and cheek. "Can't take you out in public," he scolded.

I offered to do dishes but was turned down. He scraped, not that there was much food left, and put them to soak. We settled back down in the living area to finish our wine—it took three hours. We talked like we'd never talked before. Sure, we knew each other well, but there were gaps in that knowing. I will never know if it was the salmon or the wine or the feeling of being cozy inside while it was cold outside, but something had loosened both our tongues.

I heard about his childhood and his young resentment of Maddie because she was so perfect. He was good at basketball—no surprise there—but not football and hated the latter because he didn't want to get hurt. "My kid will never play football," he vowed, and I was glad. Wait? Why am I glad? It wouldn't affect me.

I told him things I'd never said out loud before about my engagement and jilting—is that a word? My feelings came out as I considered the truth. Finally, I said, "It would have been a disastrous marriage from the get-go. As my mom always says, God works in mysterious ways. This time, he saved me." Patrick made sympathetic murmurs but never moved to comfort me by holding my hand or putting his arm around my shoulders.

He didn't ask "the" question about my relationship with the jock, and I was glad. Nor did I ask about previous girlfriends. I knew there weren't any current ones. That gap in our knowing was left open.

It was nearing midnight when I thanked him again for the surprise and the meal and headed toward my apartment.

"Pretty cold to ride bikes tomorrow," he said. "But maybe we could go for a long walk in the morning?"

I hesitated. "I've about decided to go to church in the morning. I've been promising my mom."

"Great. I'll go with you. My mom would be thrilled. What church?"

"United, on Fifty-Third. The eleven o'clock."

"Let's walk. If we leave at ten thirty or a bit before, we should be in plenty of time."

Well, that would kill Mom's basic reason for wanting me in church. I'd not meet any nice young men if Patrick was with me. But I couldn't say that, and I didn't want to.

My dreams that night were not full of Patrick. The overstuffed jock paraded before me in my sleep. Guess it was God's way of reminding me how lucky I was.

* * *

The wind off the lake the next morning was strong and cold. We decided against walking to church, and Patrick drove, finding a parking place less than a block away. We hurried, just to get out of that wind.

The church sat on the corner of Fifty-Third and Blackstone, its massive font doors in a bell tower angled exactly toward the corner. Inside, it was a bit worn—a few cracks in the paint, seat cushions that were faded and fraying. But the stained-glass windows were magnificent and, cold as it was, the sun was bright and streaming through the various colored panels. I'd tell Mom it felt good to be in church again—that would make her happy.

We were early, so we sat in silence as the congregation gradually drifted in. People sat scattered through a sanctuary obviously meant to hold more than were in attendance, and I saw only a few young families. We appeared to be the only young singles, although most looking at us would have thought we were a couple. Most of the worshippers had gray air. That probably explained the worn look of the sanctuary—the congregation was aging out.

The minister was young, not much older than Patrick and me. He began his sermon with the familiar words, "May the words of my mouth and the meditations of my heart be acceptable in thy sight, O Lord, my rock and my redeemer." Then, as the holiday was approaching, he preached on Thanksgiving. The service had begun with a hymn I'd never heard before, so I was relieved when the closing hymn was "Amazing Grace."

We went out the front door so we could shake hands with the minister—Dr. James Pullman, who did not look old enough to have doctor in front of his name.

"New to the neighborhood?" he asked, and I detected a note of hopefulness in his tone.

"Sort of," I murmured.

"Well, I certainly hope you'll visit us again. And I hope you filled out the visitor's card in the pew."

We hadn't, but I didn't tell him that. "We'll be back," I said and meant it, at least at that time. Then I realized I had no right to speak for Patrick.

Patrick was silent on the way home, so I was too. But as he parked the car, I said, "Thanks for going with me."

He turned toward me, started to say something, and then suddenly cupped my face in his hands and kissed me—hard. Not the brotherly kiss on the cheek I might have expected but the kind of kiss every girl wants from the man of her dreams. Right there, in a parked car, on Cornell Avenue. I answered loud and clear.

When we drew apart, I stared at him and finally managed a questioning, "Patrick?"

"I've wanted to do that for a long time," he said.

Wait for it, because of course I spoiled the tender moment. "But you're waiting for the right guy to come along!"

"Whaaat?" he literally yelled. "What in the hell are you talking about, Henrietta James?"

I retreated a bit, huddling in the corner of the car. "Aren't you gay?" I asked softly.

He threw his hands up in the air. "Where did you get that idea?"

I hesitated. Where did I get it? I could hardly say, "Because you're so good-looking." How about, "You're polite." Maybe, "You didn't try to seduce me." I settled for a variation of the latter.

He sighed loudly. "I thought you were fragile. You'd just been, ah, jilted at the altar—or almost so—and you kept saying you were through with men. I hoped you'd come around, but nothing ever changed. So this weekend I decided to be more forward about my feelings. Haven't you noticed?"

"I sure noticed you spent a lot more time with me than usual. I liked it."

"That's all?" His look suggested I had just hurt his feelings.

"No, that's not all. Would you kiss me again?"

The kiss lasted a long time, but we did pull apart eventually. Patrick had turned off the motor, and the car was getting cold. "Let's go inside," I said.

At the door to my apartment, he turned uncharacteristically formal. "Is it okay if I come in?"

"Of course." We never thought about lunch. Our thoughts were elsewhere, and we spent the afternoon exploring this surprising new relationship between us. Both of us were taken back a bit and yet kind of glowing with happiness. Patrick was the one who about five thirty said, "I'm starving. What's in your freezer?"

We ended up with a concoction I invented out of a can of black beans, a can of diced tomatoes, a lot of grated cheddar, and some spices. Since a fried egg makes everything better, I plopped eggs on top of both servings, and we ate with relish.

I had totally put Irene and Gabrielle out of my mind, but as I ate, reality came back. I would have to be on North Clarendon tomorrow morning. My fork clattered to the table, and I drew in a sharp breath.

Patrick was instantly concerned, putting his hand over mine. "Second thoughts?" he asked.

"Yes. About Irene."

Chapter Twenty-Two

On the bus ride Monday morning, I still felt like I was in a dream, even if the bus and Irene and Gabrielle were very real. It was one of those, "Pinch me—am I dreaming?" moments. But reality closed in when I knocked on Irene's door.

She opened it with, "Thank God you're here. I don't know what to do about Gabrielle."

The first response that came to mind was, "Not my circus, not my monkey," but I knew better than that. "How can I help?"

"By talking some sense into her." Irene led the way to our work spot as she talked.

Gabrielle had beaten us there. She sat as usual, slumped so low in the chair it was a wonder she didn't just slide right off onto the floor, a scowl on her face.

"Morning, Gabrielle." That earned me an eye roll, but as they say, I persisted. "You look unhappy. What's the matter?"

She nodded her head at Irene. "Ask her."

"I asked you."

"She has to tell me who my *real* father is."

I was glad Howard wasn't around to hear that, though I doubt he ever felt Gabrielle was much of a daughter.

"Never," Irene said through tightly clenched teeth. "I shall go to my grave with that secret."

Whoa! I thought that was carrying it too far, but before I could say anything, Gabrielle shoved her chair back from the table and abruptly stood. "I will find out long before that. And if you don't tell me, I'll ruin your career. You and your precious cooking show." With those words, she stomped back toward the bedroom area.

When I thought she was out of earshot, I asked, "Irene, why won't you tell her if it's that important to her?"

"Because he's a bad person. I was young and foolish, but now I see him for what he was, and I will not let him ruin her life. He would overindulge her."

A little late to worry about that, I thought. I decided to be bold. "Irene, I don't think you're telling me everything you know. If you want me to protect you and Gabrielle, you have to be totally honest with me."

"I never asked you to protect us. I have simply confided in you because I had no one else. If it's a burden, I shall cease."

Her tone was ever-so-haughty, and I realized I'd gone about it the wrong way. It would do no good to point out that she seemed to want me to take over all that Howard had done for her. Nor was it smart to admit that I felt a protective loyalty to her, in spite of her difficult temperament. I gave up and pulled out a chair. "Shall we get work?" I asked Irene.

She was visibly shaking with anger, and when she sat down, she sat so hard she banged her cast on the table. The tremor had jumped to her right hand.

"Irene, when does your cast come off? When do you see the doctor again?"

She shrugged. "I haven't seen him since Howard was killed. I have no way to get there."

If that was a pointed hint, I ignored it. But it did make me realize that Irene had never driven a car as long as I'd known her. I just never thought about it. Now, I was sure Gabrielle didn't drive either—and wouldn't take her mother to the doctor if she did. "Can you not Uber there?" After all, she'd been taking Uber to the studio, and I thought by now she had a favorite driver.

Again, the shrug. "I suppose so."

"Let me make you an appointment." Howard had given me the doctor's information but making the appointment was as far as I was willing to go. She agreed, and I made a note to do that later. I moved on to yet another difficult topic. The thought flashed through my mind that I wanted to shout and sing and dance, but instead we were going to talk about finances. I had no idea what Irene's reaction would be if I told her I was suddenly in love with the young man she thought so wonderful. But I was afraid I knew what her reaction would be to a financial discussion.

"Irene, we need to understand the financing of the show, who paid for what, how you got paid. The bank statements you sent me were helpful, but they didn't give the whole picture. What I think I know is that Howard paid for the studio and productions—groceries, my salary, etc.—and then sold or leased the show, under contract, to the network. And the network paid you, or paid Howard."

"They paid Howard for my services. I never had anything to do with the money. Howard took care of it all."

"Here's another question: each month, Howard deposited a hefty check in his account, with no indication where it came from. But those monthly checks stopped a while ago. Do you know who was behind them?"

Did her face really blanch for just a moment? Had I caught her off guard?

"No," she said quickly. "As I said, Howard took care of everything. I knew nothing about it."

"Are you prepared to take over the finances now?"

"John Wilson will do that. I believe he's the trustee."

That didn't mean, to me, that he'd buy the groceries! I'd have to talk to him, but that was another line I drew. I wasn't taking over the finances. I asked about the gun charges, and she said John was taking care of that. Poor John!

"There's one more thing. Penny Aldrich has reared her head again. She's taken the cookbook idea to Ina Faye Clark and is trying to publish under her name."

Instantly, "My recipes?"

"I don't know that. But I have taken steps to copyright the cookbook in your name. May I leave you a copy of what I've done so far? It's a short biography and a rough table of contents. I need you to make some notes for an introduction. I'll write it, but I need ideas from you. It will be over your signature."

I handed her the slim sheaf of papers, and she took them almost eagerly. We finally focused on the show we were to tape Wednesday afternoon. I proposed it was time for a fish dish, but of course she objected at first that not everyone ate fish. I countered, though, that many did but did not know how to cook it. So she proposed Dover sole, which is too delicate for a beginning fish cook. I countered with salmon, always a reliable choice. She chose to roast the salmon and serve it with an herb salsa and potatoes Lyonnaise. That would keep me busy in my kitchen all day tomorrow, but it sounded good. I'd take some home for me and Patrick. That nearly rolled off my tongue, but I stopped myself.

By the time we settled the details, it was time for me to leave to catch the bus. I promised to call with the doctor's appointment information and assured her she could call if she needed me.

As I was walking to the bus stop, head hunched down to avoid that persistent wind, I heard footsteps behind me and turned. Gabrielle was running after me, her mood totally changed. "I'm counting on you," she said. "Irene will never tell me about my father, but you can find him. I found this."

She thrust a newspaper clipping into my hands, and I tucked it away, unread. "Where did you find it?"

"Tucked away beneath her lingerie. I looked when she was asleep."

Gabrielle would apparently stoop to anything. I just nodded and walked on, but I was aware she stood watching me.

* * *

I resisted looking at the clipping on the bus, feeling furtive as though someone might see me. But the minute I got home, I threw down my things, fished it out of my purse, and carefully unfolded it. It was from *The New York Times,* the recent obituary of a French billionaire named Remy Charpentier. He had died of natural causes at the age of eighty-eight in Aix-en-Provence, a famous city in the south of the country. According to the obituary, Monsieur Charpentier had many business interests—a vineyard with an associated luxury hotel, a transportation company that provided luxury travel for tourists, a four-star Michelin restaurant, a large farm with a prize herd of Limousin cattle, and an art gallery in Paris. He was noted for his benevolence, supporting many charities, especially those that helped disadvantaged young people. Charpentier, a widower, was survived by one son, Chance Charpentier, who had taken over his father's financial empire several years earlier.

A bit of internet research showed me that Chance is a common first name for French males. It means "lucky" or "gambler." I'd say this Chance was lucky, and, if a gambler, he'd hit the jackpot. I looked up the father in *Forbes* and while he wasn't quite in Jeff Bezo's category, he was up among the rarified. One search led to another, and I spent the rest of the afternoon reading about Charpentier's many enterprises, seeing pictures of his several homes—one on the Riviera, a condo in New York, a mansion with sweeping views in Aux-en-Provence, and a cabin—if you use the word loosely—in a wooded rural area in France.

So now I had a clue, but what did I do with it? Monsieur Charpentier was almost definitely not Irene's long-ago lover. Age ruled him out. Besides, if he were dead, she might not be so fierce about what an evil man he was. That pointed to the son, but still left a great gap in what we knew. Chance was in all probability Gabrielle's father. But ßhow did Irene go from Chance to Howard so quickly? And how would Howard have even met Irene?

On a hunch, I went back to the Wharton website and tried to look up the graduating class of 1994, only to remember that I had to call to get information before. A quick look at my watch told me it was four thirty in Chicago, so it would be five thirty in Pennsylvania and the school offices would be closed. I'd have to wait until tomorrow.

But the more I thought about it, the more my theory made sense: Howard and Chance had met at Wharton, and when Howard went to France the summer of 2000, he visited the Charpentier family. Even if I placed Chance at Wharton, what did I do next?

"You confront Irene," Patrick said that night when I recounted the day's happenings to him. He had come straight into my apartment and into my arms when he came home about six.

"Still love me?" he asked.

"Hmmm, yes," I said just before he kissed me. Then I drew back and asked, "No late lab tonight?"

He laughed out loud. "Good one, Henny. You always know how to ruin a romantic moment."

My fridge was almost empty since I had to shop for the show first thing in the morning, so I fixed us BLT sandwiches, and Patrick fetched a nice bottle of sauvignon blanc. I promised him a roast salmon dinner Wednesday night.

"Uh, I may pick up a game tomorrow," he said, almost tentatively, "but I'll be home by eight."

Somehow with our altered relationship, his basketball didn't bother me so much. I promised to be patient.

"Okay, now tell me the latest from Clarendon Avenue."

And that's when he told me what I should have done. I usually hate being scolded for something I did or didn't do, but in this case, hindsight told me was exactly right—sort of.

"If I confront, she'll just clam up."

"Wow. Just think what a burden she must carry if she's that bitter. She needs to let go of it."

"Ha! You tell her that."

"Could you check with the Palmer House? Would they release the names of visitors?"

"Doubt it. But you know that hotel prides itself on its history. They even have a small museum and an on-staff historian—at least that's what they call him. I wonder if he'd remember a French visitor . . . and if he'd talk to me."

"They have an international reputation. They probably get a lot of guests from France."

"Still worth a try. We're not taping until four Wednesday. I could go to the Palmer House for an early lunch, maybe take their history tour."

"Henny James, are you planning to pretend an interest in history to pick that man's mind?"

"Pretend? I think it's fascinating. You know I love Chicago history."

He gave me a quick kiss on the nose. "Let's get these dishes out of the way." He rinsed, and I loaded the dishwasher, because like a lot of cooks, I'm fussy about how my dishwasher is loaded.

Tuesday was a busy day. I hit Whole Foods early before it got crowded, buying all the supplies we needed for the salmon dinner. As a bonus, I bought a couple of servings of fresh sugar snap peas I happened to discover. Then I rushed home to cook and pack the raw materials I'd take to the studio.

But as I cooked, my mind worked busily on my script for a visit to the Palmer House. I had called to make reservations for a noon lunch in what passed for their casual dining area and then I signed up for the one o'clock history tour.

I did take time off from cooking to call Wharton, where I hit the jackpot. Chance Charpentier had received an MBA in 1994. Records showed that he still resided in France. So maybe he was the man Irene met for lunch at the Palmer House, but if she hated him why would she meet him? All I could guess was that it was her twisted idea of protecting Gabrielle. And the fact that they apparently had been arguing made sense. And maybe, just maybe, he was the man she'd met for that mysterious appointment the day she broke her arm. But somehow shoving her off the curb didn't fit with my mental image of Chance Charpentier, scoundrel though he might be.

By Wednesday morning, I had my speech pretty well set, and I was excited about my adventure.

Chapter Twenty-Three

Thinking ahead is not always my strong suit, but as I packed food for the show this Wednesday morning, it occurred to me that I couldn't leave salmon, fresh and cooked, in the car for at least two hours while I sleuthed in the Palmer House. Besides, valet parking at that upscale hotel would probably break the budget permanently. I drove to the studio, early enough that I was ahead of the ten o'clock taping, which was the first one for the day. I quickly stashed everything in Irene's refrigerator—the crew knew it was off limits and they couldn't go prowling for their lunch in it. Then I requested an Uber and headed for the Palmer House.

It was barely ten thirty when I took the ground-floor elevator to the elegant and sumptuous hotel lobby. The hotel has a romantic history, built in 1871 by entrepreneur Potter Palmer as a wedding present for his bride, Bertha Honoré Potter. It was barely completed when it was destroyed by the Great Chicago Fire, along with most of downtown and many other areas. Palmer rebuilt, and his family lived in spacious apartments on the twelfth floor for several years. Palmer was one of the leaders—robber barons, if you will—of

Chicago in the late nineteenth century, but his wife, Cissy, as she was known, joked about being married to an innkeeper.

In the mid-twentieth century, the Palmer House became a Hilton hotel, which it still is today. But it retains the elegance that Palmer decreed for it. Way early for lunch, I spent a few minutes gawking at the interior. Conversational seatings of three or four chairs each were overwhelmed in a massive room with tall arches and an elaborate frescoed ceiling. Gilt seemed everywhere I looked, as I mostly gazed upward. The vast space was totally quiet, despite two couples amiably chatting in one corner. You'd have to had to shout to make a noise in this space.

Finally, my senses saturated, I pulled out the book I'd been smart enough to bring along. I'd been wanting to read—*Once Upon a Chef*, by Jennifer Segal. Segal, a trained chef, created a popular blog that offered practical, everyday recipes and cooking hints. I thought I might find some ideas for Irene, and sure enough I did. I got so lost in the book that noon came as a surprise, and I hurried downstairs to the Lockwood Restaurant & Bar, a luxurious space of dark gold walls, floor-to-ceiling drapes, and wood panel-enclosed booths. Lunch for me was cream of potato soup and a small baby salad with something called rooftop honey dressing. The server described it as a vinaigrette infused with honey from the hives on top of several downtown skyscrapers—a whole hidden industry I knew nothing about. I'm a bit reluctant about honey dressings, but this was refreshing rather than cloying.

Just shy of one o'clock, I made my way to the so-called museum, a small, glass-encased room on the mezzanine that looked out over the grand lobby. Apparently the first tourist to arrive, I waited just a few minutes for the historian, Ray Peterman, to unlock the door. Peterman had been with the hotel for many years, so I wasn't expecting a young man but wasn't quite prepared for a man probably in his seventies who was both handsome and ebullient.

I knew better than to ask my questions right off, so I oohed and aahed over the various items in that crowded little room. At first, it seemed to contain a hastily thrown together collection of junk, mostly papers, in no particular order. But gradually I made sense out of maps and menus and signed celebrity photos and artifacts such as doorknobs and ashtrays, a small model train, a silver water pitcher, even samples of fabric. Peterman was only too happy to explain the importance of each object, and I was enjoying studying the various items. He even let me turn the handle on an antique gramophone. As I browsed, other people trickled in until we were a group of ten. Peterman began his introductory lecture on the history of the hotel, dwelling lovingly on the exquisite details Mr. Palmer insisted upon.

The tour itself took us through the hotel, starting at the lobby, where he went into details about the frescoed ceiling. Then on to the grand ballroom, the Red Lacquer Room, which was astonishingly red from carpet and wall covering to the bouquets of roses set on red tablecloths. We saw a typical guest room, the gift shop, the fitness room and swimming pool, and finally ended back at the museum. We must have walked a mile, and we all sank into chairs with a sigh. Peterman answered a few questions, but one by one the guests moved on. Some lingered for private questions, and I hung back until I was the only one.

"Mr. Peterman," I began with a little flattery, "that was such an interesting tour. I read somewhere that Mrs. Palmer was a great art collector and particularly liked the French Impressionists." Yes, I had done a bit of homework late the night before.

"They were both collectors and amassed an outstanding collection, most of it in museums now. We have only a few pieces now, but the influence of the art lingers on in the décor of the hotel."

"I was wondering if you get many visitors from France, because of those early ties."

I was nothing if not devious.

"I don't know if French visitors even know about the Palmer paintings," he chuckled, "but we do get a lot of them. They like the luxury of the hotel."

"I recently read the obituary of a French billionaire named Charpentier. Does that name ring a bell?"

He rolled his eyes heavenward. "Oh, my, yes. Monsieur Charpentier was a regular visitor. He and I became good friends. I was and am terribly saddened by his death, though God knows he had a good and full life."

"Did he have investments that brought him to Chicago?"

His voice was soft. "Oh, no. His granddaughter grew up here. He came to see her, though he never visited her directly. He'd find out her schedule and watch her play in the park or walk with her nanny. I think he must have bribed the nanny, though I never would ask, but he always knew where to go to observe her. He worried about the child a lot."

"Such a sad story," I said, for once telling the outright truth. It was sad to think of that old man watching Gabrielle grow and no doubt seeing how difficult she was. I doubted the nanny had an easy time. It was also scary to think how easily the man found out the child's schedule. What if he'd wanted to kidnap her? "Does any of his family still come to see the child?"

"Oh no. That's part of the sadness. I doubt his wife knew of the child, but he told me once his son wanted nothing to do with her. Besides, she's grown now."

I had it! I had the clue I needed. But now what do I do with it? "So the son has never been here."

He shook his head, "No. Why are you so interested in this?"

I backed off. "I'm a sucker for sad stories," I said. "But I also love history, and I really enjoyed your stories today and the tour. I guess my dream is to dine in the Red Lacquer Room. But until I get to do that, may I come back sometime and hear more of your stories?" I knew I wouldn't do that, but I wanted to make him feel good.

"Of course, of course. Any time. I'll be glad to see you."

We shook hands, and I went back to the ground floor to wait for my Uber.

On the way to the studio, my head was spinning. Part of me knew that I should take this information to Detective Schmidt. He had resources I didn't and could probably even arrange to interrogate Chance Charpentier long distance. Maybe even to subpoena hotel records to find out who the Frenchman was that Irene argued with. I doubted it was Chance himself, just because of the intensity of Irene's bad feelings about him.

But going to the detective seemed to me a betrayal of Irene. It would expose her secret to the world. If I wanted to save Irene, public humiliation was not the way to do it. Selfishly, I wanted to be the one to figure this out. Somehow it was a gift I could give Irene.

Perhaps I should call John Wilson. I was going to have to call him sooner or later, but I didn't know if I should stick to business matters or should divulge this new information.

As the Uber pulled into the studio parking lot, I had a revelation: The senior Charpentier must be the one who sent Howard money every month. When he died, the son cut off the payments.

By the time I walked into the studio, I was worn out. I wanted nothing more than a nap.

* * *

Another day when taping didn't go well, but this time the fault was all mine. I was emotionally exhausted, and my mind was anywhere but on roasted salmon. I was slow on the uptake, rather than anticipating what Irene needed before she knew she needed it. Once I handed her pre-measured sugar instead of salt—fortunately it was only a tiny bit. But I decided then and there that I would take home the pre-cooked fish and leave Irene's version for the crew. Ken had to stop the shooting twice because either I flubbed or I made Irene so nervous she did. Finally, he called, "It's a wrap." I swear I heard him mutter under his breath, "Sort of."

The minute the cameras were off us, Irene turned on me. "It is that charming young man, isn't it? You're not getting enough sleep!" She pronounced this with all the French savor of romance she could muster, and Emily Dickinson's lines went through my mind, "Wild nights, wild nights/Were I with thee/Wild nights should be/Our luxury." I hated to disappoint her by saying that no, Patrick was not keeping me up, but I was worried about something.

She instantly turned on the kind, solicitous side of her. "Is it something I can help with? You know, *chérie*, you can always talk to me. I rely on you so much now that dear Howard is gone. And I know he would want me to do whatever I can to help you."

I wanted to shout, "Of course you can help me! Tell me the truth about Gabrielle's father and your relationship with him." But that would cut off any hope I had of ever getting the truth out of her, so I said, "No, Madame, but thank you. It will work itself out." My mind even then was wondering, "But how?"

She shook her head sympathetically. "If I can ever help, you come to me. I am expert in matters of the heart."

So now she thought we'd had a lovers' quarrel. Patrick would howl when he heard that, but I was not amused.

Finally, I shoveled her into her Uber and climbed into my car, headed for home. Once there, I dumped my groceries, stuck the salmon in the fridge and headed for bed. It was eight o'clock, and I figured Patrick was playing basketball. As I drifted off, I hoped maybe he'd go for beer with his buddies.

No such luck. About ten o'clock, he woke me with gentle shaking. "Hey, you can't be asleep. We have to talk."

My brain was so foggy that I asked, "Why? Did something happen at the university today? You see a special star?"

He laughed. "No, you're the star. I want to know about the history tour at the Palmer House."

How could I forget? The day gradually came back to me. Before I could speak, he practically pulled me out of bed and stood me on the floor, steadying me with gentle hands and turning me toward the kitchen. "You want coffee?"

I shook my head. Coffee was the last thing I wanted. Sleep was first on that list. All my excitement about what I'd learned seemed to have slipped away while I slept.

Patrick opened a beer for himself and waved a wine bottle at me, but I declined. "Could I have a cold glass of water?"

Finally, my water poured, he sat down at the table expectantly. "Okay, lay it on me."

And I did. I gathered a little steam as I described my encounter with Ray Peterman and the confirmation—well, almost positive—that Gabrielle was the granddaughter of French billionaire Remy Charpentier.

"Wow! Henny, you've solved it. You've found the answer." He was at this point more excited than I was.

"To the question of who Gabrielle's biological father is, but not who killed Howard and why. Who was the man Irene met at the Palmer House? I don't think it was Gabrielle's father. And why won't Irene tell any of us the truth?"

"That one's fairly obvious. Irene was scorned in love, and she's bitter."

I couldn't hide a smile. "Today she decided first that you and I were having some wild affair, and I wasn't getting enough sleep . . . "

He did. He actually leered at me.

I ignored him and went on. "Then she decided we were having a lovers' quarrel, and that's why my mind wasn't on what I was doing today. Told me she was an expert at matters of the heart. Made me wonder how she could be if her experience was being jilted once and rebounding immediately to Howard. I mean, they loved each other a great deal—I've always believed that—but I never thought of it as a passionate romance."

"Maybe in their youth?"

"Remember, she was, as they say, big with child. I really think it was a business arrangement. Gabrielle's grandfather paid Howard, maybe not so much to take care of Irene as to take care of his granddaughter."

"Did he have any other grandchildren?"

I shook my head. "The obituary listed the son as the only survivor."

"So now what?"

"That's what I don't know, but I'm not going to figure it out. I'm going back to bed." And I left him sitting at the table. Maybe, I thought, inspiration would come in my dreams.

It didn't.

Chapter Twenty-Four

Thursday was to be a research day for me, with the understanding Irene would call if she needed something or had an idea. Then Friday, I would trek back up to North Clarendon for sort of a conference to see where we stood, what we'd accomplished during the week. But Thursday morning, I could look forward to a peaceful day, even though I knew my thoughts would wander all over the place trying to decide how to find out more about the Charpentier family and the identity of the man Irene had now twice met—or so I suspected. It turned out to be anything but a peaceful day that took my thoughts away from the Charpentier puzzle.

About ten thirty in the morning, the production manager at the TV station called. I'd never had a thing to do with the station, so I was totally unprepared for this.

"Ms. James, my name is Bob Thorne. I just talked to Mrs. Foxglove, but she referred me to you, says you're handling the business end of her cooking show."

Warily, I agreed. It was, after all, true in practice if not part of my job description.

He didn't mince words. Over the phone his voice was deep, the tone clearly antagonistic. "We've had a complaint that Mrs. Foxglove has falsified her credentials. We've long advertised the show as featuring a chef trained in France at Le Cordon Bleu. I was told today that is not true. She never was in France."

Penny Aldrich had tried one more time. If she had been the murder victim instead of Howard, I would have been a likely suspect. "Who told you that?"

He was smooth. "I'm sorry. My source must remain anonymous."

Hardly fair, I thought, but I plunged ahead. "I know your source. It was a woman named Penny Aldrich." Inspiration struck. "She may have given a male identity. Her voice is very deep."

"That's neither here nor there," he said. "I need to verify Mrs. Foxglove's training, and I figure it's your responsibility, not mine. I see no need for me to hire a translator and deal with a French cooking school."

I was quite confident they spoke English at Le Cordon Bleu, but that too was beside the point. "I can assure you she was in France at the turn of this century. She was an au pair, helping with various housework, including cooking, for the famed French family, the Charpentiers." He wouldn't know if they were famed or not, but it sounded good.

"I need to see something on paper," he insisted. "From Le Cordon Bleu."

"I don't have such at hand, but I'll see what I can do."

"We want to be reasonable," he said, "and I know overseas transactions can be timely. Shall we say you'll get back to me in a week?"

"A week," I muttered.

After Mr. Thorne abruptly disconnected the call, I sat and thought about options. The trouble was that I didn't really believe that Irene had been trained at the Cordon Bleu. It didn't fit into the timeline I had mentally developed for her. It must have been summer 2000 when, still an au pair, she found herself pregnant, confronted Chance Charpentier, who refused to claim responsibility, and threw herself on the mercy of the elder Charpentier, Remy. At the same time, Howard, touring Europe on his dream vacation, stopped in Aix-en-Provence to visit Chance. Chance probably told him the crazy American wanted to blackmail him, but Howard, basically a good guy, may have sympathized with Irene. Watching these young people interact, Monsieur Charpentier had taken Howard aside and offered him the deal of a lifetime: marry this girl and raise my grandchild appropriately, and I will support you for life. Trouble came because Monsieur did not put that clause in his will, and Chance cut off the payments on his father's death. Perhaps Howard threatened to go public—or even Irene, though that would have spilled the secret to Gabrielle. Maybe there was another threat Howard could hold over his head. None of that speculation, however, helped with my immediate problem—a certificate from Le Cordon Bleu.

On a hunch, I booted my computer and went to the site for the Kendall College. The school's subsidiary, the Kendall School of Cooking, offered a BA in culinary arts or an associate degree, the latter guaranteed to prepare students for a career in the culinary world. I called the registrar's office.

"This is Henrietta James, publicity manager for Irene Foxglove and her TV show." That was a stretch maybe but not really an untruth. "We want to be sure to credit her training at Kendall College. Can you tell me what year she received the associate degree in the culinary arts?"

Whoever answered the phone sounded young and probably blessedly green, not quite up to privacy protection. The word publicity probably got her. "Oh, goodness. Just let me check. I've watched her show, and I do admire her."

Bonus! A fan, sort of.

In a minute she was back on the line. "Mrs. Foxglove took an accelerated program and received her degree in the summer of 2001."

"Really? She must have been enthusiastic to go through so rapidly. When did she enroll?"

Silence for a minute, and then, "The fall of 2000."

I hoped I wasn't pushing my luck when I asked, "Under the name Foxglove?"

"No, ma'am. She first registered as Irene Lindberg, but a notation says she changed it to Foxglove in November of that year. You will be sure to send us a copy of the publicity, won't you?"

I assured her I would and hung up. There was no need to call Cordon Bleu in France. I had my answer. I just didn't know what to do with it. One thought that came to me was that perhaps now I had an idea about the beginning of Gabrielle's strained relationship with her mother. They had never really bonded when Gabrielle was an infant, because Irene had been too busy at culinary school. I envisioned the nanny nurturing that baby.

After a lot of mulling it over, doodling on a legal pad, writing Irene Lindberg over and over, I had an idea. My email to Bob Thorne began with thanks for his inquiry and the opportunity to correct a misunderstanding.

"Mrs. Foxglove is devastated that the information she supplied was somehow misinterpreted and is anxious to correct it. What she told her former publicist, Penny Aldrich, is that she is a proud graduate of Kendall College here in Chicago, but prior to moving to Chicago, she had the opportunity to study in the private kitchens of two French chefs who had trained at Cordon Bleu. She was at that time an au pair in the household of Monsieur Remy Charpentier and arrangements were made through her employer."

Okay, it was a white lie, but I figured Thorne would never follow up on the French chefs. The only loose end left was Penny Aldrich. She had to be stopped once and for all. I took care of that with a quick call to John Wilson, who said he would send a "cease and desist" letter to Penny and threaten her with a harassment lawsuit.

At the end of the day, I was quite proud of what I'd accomplished, even if I hadn't done much research. I had managed to pull together three recipes for Irene's consideration—a choucroute, which she would accept because it is a French dish even as she scorned it as peasant food. I'd remind her that some of those cooking from her book might be the American equivalent of the French peasant. Quail stuffed with white grapes would be much more to her liking, Days earlier I had pulled a ham recipe—ham steaks marinated and broiled in the oven. The dish would give Irene a chance to advise cooks knowledgeably on the advantages of buying a whole ham and having the butcher cut off steaks, leaving the rest for a variety of other uses.

In fact, that night, because I already had the ham, I made Patrick a cheesy gougère ring with creamed ham and peas in the center. As I cooked, I decided I'd brain him with a skillet if he played basketball and let my gougère fall flat. It should be eaten right out of the oven. But he didn't disappoint. He was at my door asking what smelled so good by six, and I had to make him sip on a glass of white wine as I finished up the main dish and made a salad.

We had a lovely evening.

* * *

Next morning I was on the bus, laden with my backpack filled with legal pad, computer, and other papers. By just a few minutes after ten, I buzzed the apartment from the lobby and headed upstairs.

Irene's greeting was getting tiresome. "I'm glad you're here," she said through tight lips.

Anticipating her problem, I asked, "Gabrielle?"

"She's gone," she said, nearly making me drop the backpack I'd just taken off my shoulders.

Brushing past her to the dining table, I muttered, "I have to sit down." Then, after I caught my breath, "Tell me what happened."

She shrugged. "I don't know. She was gone when I woke up yesterday." She had seated herself at the table across from me, sitting as erect as ever. I didn't detect any tears, not even a lot of worry. Just a certain puzzlement.

I was floored. "Yesterday? You didn't call me?" Didn't take me long to realize that was a blessing for me, but I worried about her alone all day yesterday, not knowing what to do. She apparently did nothing to find her daughter for twenty-four hours, even a bit more.

"What could you do?" she asked.

I shrugged. "You didn't call Detective Schmidt?"

"You and I both know the police don't pay attention for twenty-four hours. I thought we should call him this morning." Then she added, "Howard would have known what to do."

The collective pronoun was not lost on me. She was waiting for me to take charge, to take some action. By herself, she was adrift.

* * *

Detective Schmidt was almost at the door before I could disconnect my phone call, and that's only a slight exaggeration. But it gave me time to flash back two days to the Palmer House. Instinct told me the hotel was involved. Too much revolved around it, but telling Detective Schmidt about it would amount to confessing I'd been sleuthing on my own and keeping knowledge from him—specifically the identity of the Charpentier family. And I'd have to do that in front of Irene.

I let Irene tell her part of the story, which really wasn't much.

"I have no idea where she could have gone or why. She did not take clothes, doesn't answer her cell phone."

Schmidt fired rapid questions at her, and Irene responded calmly. No, she wasn't on any medications. No, she had not taken much if any of her makeup with her. Yes, there were tensions between them. No, they didn't talk about it. Finally, he threw up his hands in exasperation and said, "What are you not telling me?"

It was my chance. With a swift glance at Irene, I said, "Detective, the problem between them has to do with the identity of Gabrielle's biological father."

Irene stiffened, but I plunged ahead. "I now know his identity, and I may have some helpful information." I explained about the Charpentier family, keeping an eye always on Irene. She bit her lip, drummed her hand on the table, and shifted nervously in her chair. But she kept quiet.

"You remember the man Irene had lunch with at the Palmer House?"

At this, Irene jumped up. "How would he remember him? How did you even know I went to the Palmer House? Have you been spying on me?" Her angry stare went back and forth between the detective and me.

"Madame," I said in my most tactful tone, "we both knew you weren't telling us everything."

"Why should I?" she demanded. "A person has a right to keep some things in life private."

"Not when a murder is involved," Detective Schmidt said. He was almost but not quite gentle, and I blessed him for not flaring in anger.

"If I may continue," I said, "I went to the Palmer House and spoke with the historian on staff. He likes to talk, and it wasn't hard to get him to share a piece of news that will interest you, Irene. Over the years, Monsieur Charpentier has come to Chicago periodically to see his granddaughter. No, they never met. He watched her from a distance."

At that, Irene's rage turned to tears. She had jumped to her feet at my initial revelation, but now she sat back in her chair, buried her face in her hands, and sobbed uncontrollably. I went to the kitchen in search of a box of tissues and brought the whole box back to her.

"He was a good man," she said between sobs. "He took care of me. Not like . . ." And she dissolved in tears again.

Schmidt, meanwhile, was apparently processing what I said, because when I re-entered the room, he said, "Wait a minute. If he observed from a distance, how did he know where the child would be, how he could watch? From what you say, he's a man of power and money. I can hardly imagine him staking this apartment out, sitting long hours in a car."

"That's just it," I said. "He didn't. He had someone do it for him. The man Irene met." I turned to her. "It's time now to tell us who he is and what you know about him. I don't think Gabrielle is in danger, but I do think your relationship with her is. If you don't want her to disappear to France, you better tell the detective what you know."

You could see defeat in the slump of her shoulders and, when she raised her head to look at us, in her eyes. All the fight had gone, and she was limp, motionless. In almost a whisper, she said, "His name is Abel Dubois. He was a—what do you call it?—right-hand man for Remy Charpentier. He is not always, ah . . . careful about his methods. He is the man who pushed me off the curb." She gestured toward the cast on her arm.

"I have a picture," Schmidt said, "not a very good one, but the tail did his best at the hotel that day. I can email it to you for identification."

Irene just nodded.

"Why did you meet with him again?" Schmidt was almost impatient.

"Because he was threatening Gabrielle. He would tell her the truth about Chance Charpentier"—she nearly spit out the name—

"but make up lies about Howard and me. He reports to Chance now, and Chance is not the gentleman his father was. It seems Chance is now alone—divorced, no legitimate children, his parents dead. Abel says he wants family, and Gabrielle is all that's left. He stopped the payments as a way of putting pressure on me and Howard." It seemed to tire her out to confess all this, and she put her head in her arms down on the table.

Detective Schmidt was stunned. "This may be the wildest criminal theory I ever heard. How do we know Gabrielle didn't just decide to leave? She may be comfortably in some hotel . . . or on a plane to France on her own. If I start a ruckus at the Palmer House, of all places, and it turns out she's just an overage runaway . . ." Words seemed to fail him at this point.

"I have no proof of any of this, just some hunches and what I learned from a talkative old man. But it makes sense to me," I offered.

"That's just the trouble. It makes sense to me. I can't ignore it, but I swear if I get demoted over this . . . I can go to the general manager and ask politely to see the hotel's guest registry. But it probably won't get me anywhere. It would be safer to get a judge's order. That will take at least twenty-four hours. And we don't know if this Dubois character used his full name or not." Another pause. "In twenty-four hours, Dubois could have whisked her off to France. I could stake out the lobby, but who knows if he'll take her to a restaurant or order room service. We don't have a good picture to give to a stakeout. And I can't exactly put an army of people in the Palmer House. One officer is all I can manage."

"If you told the manager that the hotel was involved in a possible kidnapping, perhaps to avoid scandal they would cooperate."

He shook his head. "Doubtful, but it's worth a try. I'll also start things rolling with a judge. I'll be in touch as soon as I know anything. Mrs. Foxglove," he addressed her in a gentle voice, "try not to worry. We'll get your girl back for you."

Irene raised her tear-stained face. "Thank you."

As I walked him to the door, I whispered, "Gabrielle is not always easy to deal with. Monsieur Dubois may be glad to get rid of her."

He grinned just slightly, a first for the morning. "He could do us all, including himself, a favor and bring her back home. We'd still have to go after him, though. Can't have foreigners getting away with kidnapping an American citizen."

After he left, I had a dilemma. It was barely past eleven in the morning, and I did not want to stay in that apartment the whole long day. The atmosphere was depressing, as though the walls themselves were sending out negative vibes. But could I leave Irene alone? Would she do something foolish? Harm herself? Good thing Detective Schmidt had taken the gun.

I put the kettle on to make a pot of tea.

Chapter Twenty-Five

Irene made the decision for me. I poured tea, sweetened hers with honey, just the way she liked it, and we sat in silence as we sipped. At length, she said, "I need to be alone, Henrietta. I appreciate that you are trying to help me, but now I have to think about all this." She gave a small, ironic chuckle. "It's been quite a morning."

So by twelve thirty I was back home but antsy. Patrick was gone, of course, and I couldn't concentrate on food. What I wanted to do every five minutes was to call Detective Schmidt and demand to know what was happening. As the afternoon dragged on—two o'clock, three o'clock—with no word, I worried about Irene. What was she doing? The rational part of me kept saying that Gabrielle was in no danger and Irene would never harm herself, but the imagination under stress is a powerful thing.

He called a little after four. "Did you look at the picture yet?"

I had to confess I hadn't booted up my computer, so as I listened to him, I switched it on and keyed in my password.

"The manager was cooperative, partly I think because he has a daughter about the same age, and partly because he doesn't want even a hint of scandal at his hotel. I've got an officer in there now, disguised as a food service employee. She'll respond if he calls for service for supper. I want you and Mrs. Foxglove in the hotel. Despite their relationship, the girl may need her mother. And the mother seems to rely heavily on you."

I sighed. Truer words were never spoken.

"Could you identify this Dubois fellow from the picture?"

I was looking at a grainy image of a man and woman at a restaurant table. The woman, with her back to me, was clearly Irene. The man was gesturing and talking, so it was hard to tell a lot about his face. But he was not the sophisticated Frenchman of my dreams. He was big, not fat, just big, his clean-shaven face broad, his nose crooked as though it had been broken. His hair was apparently dark, neither short nor long but a bit curly. He was not smiling, and I thought Irene brave just to be sitting across the table from him.

"Yes, I think so."

"Good. I want you to be in the Lockwood Room in case he takes the girl to dinner. I think that's where they most likely would go. My bet is on room service, but I want to cover all possibilities."

A part of me was terrified at the idea of even being close to this man, and I wanted to protest that I had not signed up for the police department.

"You clearly know the girl and can identify her and she can recognize you, but we'll have you hidden. Don't want her to walk in and demand to know what her mother's assistant is doing there." He chuckled, but I didn't think it was funny.

"Can you get down there by five? I've called Mrs. Foxglove, told her a car would pick her up. We'll stash her in the GM's office until we see what happens."

At least Irene would be safe, but I didn't feel good about my safety. I told myself this Dubois wasn't going to start waving a gun in a crowded restaurant . . . or was he? I considered breaking a strict rule of my own and calling Patrick during the day. In the end, I left him a note before I took an Uber downtown.

* * *

At the Palmer House, as instructed by Schmidt, I asked to be shown to the general manager's office. A receptionist ushered me into a small and private room furnished as a sitting room with a couch and three or four upholstered chairs. Irene was there, seated in a chair, staring into space, but clutching her purse as though she thought someone would snatch it from her. When I entered the room, she stood and, uncharacteristically, held out her arms. I walked into an unexpected hug. But she nearly walloped me in the head with her purse, because she hadn't even set it down for a hug. I wanted to reassure her that were probably no purse-snatchers in the office of the general manager of the Palmer House.

"Thank you for coming," she said, sitting down again. "I hardly know what I'm doing."

"I don't think any of us do," I said, "except for Detective Schmidt. I sure hope he does." I wasn't sure if that was a wry smile or a grimace.

The receptionist offered us coffee, tea, or wine, and we both accepted a glass of wine. The drinks had barely been delivered when Schmidt walked in, looking grimly businesslike. I sensed Irene tensing up, and I felt none too relaxed myself.

"Ladies, thank you. I hope in a couple of hours, we'll have your daughter safe, Mrs. Foxglove, and you can go home, both of you." He nodded in my direction. "Mrs. Foxglove, if you'll just remain here until I come get you, and it may be some time."

The receptionist turned out to be named Betty Peterman. I was willing to bet she was the historian's daughter, which meant nothing except that was probably how she got the job. She offered Irene magazines, but the diva dismissed them with a wave of her hand.

"I couldn't pay attention," she said.

To me, Schmidt said, "Come with me" and led the way to elevators and down to the Lockwood Restaurant. He introduced me to the hostess and led me to a booth partially hidden by a leafy fern. Motioning for me to slide into the booth, he sat across from me and handed me a makeup compact. "Here, powder your nose." He actually was grinning just a bit.

I opened it and found it was a mirror which I could angle all around and get a good view of the room.

"You can talk to it too," he said, "softly, of course. I'll be listening. Also listen for texts coming in on your phone. And study the menu a lot." He took a menu from the hostess and gave it to me, a long, tall thing that I could easily hide behind.

He thanked me and left, and the hostess went about her duties. So there I was, a woman alone in a restaurant, which didn't bother me too much. But it was only five thirty, way too early for a sophisticated Frenchman to want dinner. I saw a long, nervous evening stretching ahead for me.

I had really only had two sips of wine upstairs, so I asked for another glass of chardonnay, promising myself I would have only one. It wouldn't do to get too happy on the job, as it were. Opening the menu, I saw several appealing things and had to remind myself I probably wouldn't get to eat. The menu was heavy with Lake Michigan fish products, mostly whitefish—Lake Michigan caviar, fish sticks, fish and chips, a smoked whitefish spread. It made me think Irene should make more use of the haul from Lake Michigan. Wonder if I could talk her into it?

A waitress brought my wine and said, "Mr. Schmidt would like you to order dinner." It sounded like an order.

"Give me a minute, please." I went back to the menu with more interest and finally decided on the sea scallops served with a squash puree, asparagus, and roasted carrots. After the server took my order, I checked my watch—I had been there all of fifteen minutes.

When my phone vibrated, I nearly jumped out of my skin. Should I answer the phone or the compact? I chose the phone, expecting to hear Schmidt. I got Patrick who, most unlike him, was upset.

"Henny, what the hell are you doing? I never heard anything so foolish—at the Palmer House, be home late. What was I supposed to think? Do I need to come down there?"

Yes, no, and maybe. "Patrick, it's been a really tough day. Yes, I'd love you to come down here, but no, not now. Can you be on standby?"

"Only if you explain what you're doing. And talk up, I can barely hear you."

"I can't do either of those things. Just trust me."

"Great, just great. It will be a long evening of trusting Henny."

If he'd been in front of me, I'd have thrown the phone at him.

The scallops were tasty, but I played with my food like a picky eater. Maybe Patrick and I could have a late dinner. I checked my watch. Another twenty minutes. The evening was speeding by.

My phone vibrated again at precisely twenty-four minutes until eight.

"He ordered room service," Schmidt said. "Go back to the manager's office and wait with Irene. I'll come get you at the right time."

Irene was surprised to see me, so I gathered Schmidt hadn't called her. I filled her in briefly, but I could see that my best attempt to be reassuring didn't work.

"Gabrielle won't be hurt, will she?"

"No, of course not. Detective Schmidt will protect her. He knows what he's doing."

It was another silent wait. My phone pinged once, but it was a text from Patrick, wanting to know how much longer and was I okay. I was texting back when Schmidt himself appeared. It later occurred to me that if he'd sent an emissary, I would have refused to leave the safety of the office.

To Irene, he said tersely, "Your daughter needs you." But he said no more as we rode the elevator to the eleventh floor. Only when the doors slid open did he give us a bit of background. "We're holding Dubois in the room for Irene to make a positive identification. He'll be charged with kidnapping. Your daughter was bound in a chair and gagged." With that he strode down the hall, opened a door, and ushered us into a luxurious room.

Or what had been a luxurious room. We almost bumped into a dining service cart that nearly blocked the doorway, but as we advanced into the room I saw an unmade double bed, the covers tossed about, and a daybed that was neatly made except that the decorative pillows were thrown about. A Windsor chair was overturned as though there had been a scuffle, and newspapers were scattered on the floor.

Abel Dubois was as unpleasant in person as he had been in the picture. If Gabrielle was bound to a chair, this time it was his turn. His hands were cuffed behind him around the back of a straight chair, which he occasionally rocked as though he would overturn it. His look was nothing near subdued but more like arrogant.

But it was Gabrielle who commanded attention. She sat on the edge of the daybed, clutching a handful of tissues. Whatever makeup she had once had on was smudged, smeared, and gone. Trails of mascara marked her wet cheeks, which she tried to blot.

Her lovely long hair was a tangled mess. Most remarkable was the look on her face—to this day I can't fully describe it. Part agony, but a big part disbelief that this had happened to her. Whereas I thought she might run to her mother, their differences now forgotten and forgiven, she looked up at Irene and, in a tentative, questioning voice, said, "Mother?"

Irene began to fumble with that purse that she had refused to be parted from, and I thought she was going for more tissues—for herself, for Gabrielle. But as I stared at her I saw something shiny in her purse, and before I knew what I was doing, I yelled, "Gun!" and threw myself at her.

I caught her off-balance, and the force of my leap knocked us both to the floor. The open purse went flying, and a small gun rolled out on the floor. The room service clerk, dressed in a black-and-white outfit, apron and all, had assumed the stance of a police office, both hands out in front holding a handgun.

Simultaneously, Schmidt yelled, "Oh my God!" and in one smooth dive, picked up Irene's weapon. Pulling Irene to her feet, he handed me the gun, which I thought showed a lot of confidence.

"Mrs. Foxglove, where did you get this derringer?"

Stunned, she turned to Gabrielle. "In my daughter's bedroom. In her lingerie drawer, tucked beneath the clothing. I didn't know she had it, don't know why she had it."

I was thinking that these women needed to stop prowling in each other's lingerie drawers, when Gabrielle answered Irene's question.

"For protection."

Schmidt whirled on her, "Protection from what?"

Gabrielle shrugged. "I don't know. Everything around me seemed scary, out of balance. After Howard died, I didn't know what would happen."

"I don't suppose you have a license," Schmidt said wryly.

She nodded. "I do. I took the class and everything. The license is at home. I never carried the gun anywhere."

Irene dodged out of Schmidt's grasp and sat beside her daughter, arms outstretched. "Where you afraid of me, Gabrielle? I couldn't bear it if you were."

Gabrielle looked stricken. "No, not exactly. But you wouldn't tell me who my father was, and yet you let slip he wanted to meet me, and you kept emphasizing that he was a very bad person."

Irene put a nervous hand—her good hand—to her mouth. "I have done all this. I am the one who caused all the trouble. Not Chance. But Abel is guilty. He has done Chance's dirty work for years." She cast a look at him.

"What were you going to do with the gun?" Schmidt asked.

"Shoot Abel," she said simply. "I don't care what happens to me. If you gave it back to me right now, I would shoot him."

Abel looked a little alarmed at this, but Schmidt waved a dismissive hand. "I'm not giving her the gun," he said. Then, to his officer who still held the position, "Officer Dunbar, relax a bit. Call for backup and transportation, please. No sirens. Silent approach. We don't want to upset the Palmer House." With a glance at Gabrielle, he added, "Call the medics too, please."

Office Dunbar grinned just a bit and said, "Yessir." She left the room, presumably to use her phone in the hall. At least I hoped she didn't go any farther away. And my hope appeared timely.

She was barely outside when Dubois began rocking his chair. Schmidt just stared at him, and when the chair finally tipped, leaving Dubois still bound to it but lying on the floor, Schmidt calmly asked, "Satisfied? Did you hit your head?"

Dubois muttered an expletive.

Irene and Gabrielle sat with their arms around each other, whispering comforting phrases. It almost made me cry.

In no time at all, that good-sized hotel room was pandemonium. It seemed like an army had descended. Two officers yanked Dubois off the floor, uncuffed him just long enough to cuff him again, and marched him out the door. People took photographs, and others dusted for fingerprints. They opened every drawer, threw back bed covers, searched the bathroom. I saw some putting objects in clear plastic bags, but I couldn't see for sure what they were saving.

Detective Schmidt stood in the middle of all this confusion like a commanding general. When the medics arrived, he steered them to

Gabrielle, explained what she'd been through, and said, "Hospitalize her if you need to."

Both Gabrielle and Irene looked alarmed at that, but Schmidt softened it. "I think you'll check out okay, but we have to be sure. After the medics release you, I'll send you both home with twenty-four-hour protection. You can give your statements tomorrow."

Why twenty-four-hour protection, I wondered. Did he think Dubois had accomplices? All the activity swirling around me left me feeling useless and lost, but when I tried to leave, Schmidt called me back. "James, you need to give a statement. I'll take it soon as I can. I already got most of it."

"I just need to make a phone call," I stammered. I desperately needed Patrick.

He nodded. "Out in the hall."

Patrick said he'd be there as quickly as he could, and it was probably only forty-five minutes before he got there, but it seemed like hours. He was in the lobby, and the eleventh floor was off limits to everyone but authorized personnel—meaning police. I explained the situation to Schmidt, and he spoke into that thing on his shoulder. Within minutes, Patrick emerged from the elevator, escorted by an officer.

I threw myself at him.

"Henny, you're gonna knock us both over again," he said, as he wrapped his arms around me. I was shaking with nerves, exhaustion, I don't know what.

Schmidt came out into the hall. "That was some greeting." To Patrick, he said, "You're a lucky guy."

I squirmed, but Patrick said, "I know. Can I take her home?"

Schmidt seemed to debate with himself. Finally, he said, "Yeah. You bring her to the station tomorrow to give a statement."

Patrick's "of course" squelched my urge to protest that I would be perfectly fine in the morning and could get to the station myself. After a second thought, I decided not to speak. I wanted Patrick to be with me.

Schmidt turned impatient. "If you're gonna leave, go on and go. I got work to do."

"Irene . . . Gabrielle . . ." I protested.

"I'll give 'em your love. Go on!" And he turned and went back into the room.

Epilogue

Abel Dubois confessed not to kidnapping but to luring Gabrielle to the Palmer House with promises of a new wardrobe of her choosing, the expensive meals at restaurants she claimed her family never took her to, and a trip to France to see her father. She had, he insisted, willingly gotten into his car early in the morning after some secretive phone calls to make the arrangements. Charpentier's private jet was waiting at Midway Airport to whisk them overseas. The question of how Dubois intended to get his "difficult" guest out of the hotel and to the airport without attracting attention went unanswered, but I suspected sedation and a claim of illness. I'm sure Dubois could have spun a great—and believable—story.

The flaw in his story, of course, was that she was bound, gagged, and in tears when rescued. Dubois explained that with a Gallic gesture of dismissal, but what he said amounted to describing Gabrielle as so difficult and demanding that he could no longer listen to her. When he tried to talk sense to her—in his version—she decided that the adventure was not working out as she hoped and demanded to be taken home. He would not do that, of course, because his loyalty and obligation were to Chance Charpentier. Surely, the United States authorities understand that, *n'est-il pas si?*

The United States authorities did not agree that it was so, and there was the matter of Howard Foxglove's murder. *Oh désolé à ce sujet*, which amounts to "Sorry about that. It was a mistake." Abel had been sent to Chicago to pressure Howard and Irene to abandon their demand that the payments from the Charpentier fortune continue. He had tried at a lunch meeting with Irene, and no, he did not push her off the sidewalk. No French gentleman would do such a thing. Sending a note threatening Irene brought no response from Howard, so Dubois arranged to meet Howard that morning a block from the Clarendon apartment, which explained Howard's uncharacteristic decision to go for a walk. But instead of caving in, as Dubois expected, Howard was obstinate and went so far as to push him away. Dubois had no choice but to defend himself. Surely, the authorities could understand that, *n'est-il pas si?*

No, the authorities could not understand that. He would be formally charged with kidnapping and murder and following a judge's decision held without bail as a flight risk.

Gabrielle's version of the story differed somewhat from Abel's. She described "that man" as abusive, though to everyone's apparent relief there had been no physical abuse beyond the restraints. Pressed as to why she would willingly go with a stranger, she offered vague reasons about meeting her "real" father. "But I have never been treated that way in my life!" She seemed to think that explained everything, and the police decided to be satisfied with the sketchy statement she gave.

Irene's statement to the police was mostly about confirming the identity of Abel Dubois as an employee of the Charpentier empire. She confirmed Gabrielle's statement that he was a bully and not a gentleman and clung to her claim that he had pushed her off the curb. She had kept silent about her two meetings with him initially because she didn't want Howard to know and then because she was ashamed. She said, rather dramatically, that she tried to appeal to Dubois' better nature but now understood that he didn't have one.

It seemed that Dubois would be convicted more on his own actions than on the testimony of his accusers.

What struck me when I heard all this was that I had been right all along that Irene was keeping secrets. She knew the truth, down to Chance Charpentier's change of heart and Howard's death, but refused to tell any of us who were trying to help her. She must have been terrified, alone with her secrets.

* * *

Once again, *Cooking with Irene* skated by on reruns until the network stepped in, some two weeks after the kidnapping. I called Irene and arranged for us to meet and map out the shows we would shoot.

Perhaps I was emboldened by my role in all that had happened or maybe it was love that made me more confident, but for the first time I braved the Outer Drive. I survived the trip without accident and arrived at Irene's promptly at ten o'clock one morning.

Madame greeted me at the door with the now-familiar words, "I'm glad you're here. We need to talk." I considered screaming, "Now what?"

Irene, cast off her left arm, had put out the usual coffee and croissants. Gabrielle sat at the table, looking a little less belligerent and a little more interested in what was going on. Not that she was a changed person. She did not say good morning nor lift her eyes to meet mine, and she was already nibbling daintily on a croissant rather than politely waiting for Irene and me. I remembered how long it had once taken her to eat half a hamburger. Coffee poured and croissants in hand, we endured an awkward silence.

Finally, Irene spoke. "Gabrielle and I have many things to work out, and much difficulty lies ahead for us."

I glanced at Gabrielle and decided she looked a little bored. My hopes were up that Irene was about to announce they were going into counseling. No such luck.

"We can best do it in France."

I was floored. After I found my tongue again, I asked, "But the show . . . " No, I didn't quite say that the show must go on, but that was my thought. At least partly selfish, for my livelihood—my very reason for being in Chicago and near Patrick—depended on the show.

Irene was imperious now. "I do not need the show, and you must notify the network and cancel the studio appointments. I am going to France with my daughter. The length of our stay is not yet determined. I will put everything"—a sweeping gesture seemed to take in the entire apartment—"in storage. I am ready to begin a new life." She hesitated, as though unsure she wanted to say the next thing on her mind. I have been in touch with Chance, and he is going to buy me a small café in a town near Aix-en-Provence. We will share Gabrielle."

Share Gabrielle? As though she were a piece of pie to be divided? I saw nothing but disaster ahead, but I kept my tongue. A glance at Gabrielle confirmed a triumphant look on her face. I realized that neither one of them had learned much from all that had happened. They simply hadn't grown and changed. Had I? I hoped so.

I took a devious route back to Hyde Park, weaving through city streets. It took me two hours and gave me time to clear my head. Gabrielle had left the room, without a goodbye, as I picked up my things and got ready to leave. At the door, Irene and I had come as close to goodbyes as either of us could.

The nice side of Irene came out. She who had just uprooted my life put an affectionate arm around me—at least that's how I interpreted it—and said how indebted she was to me, how much she appreciated everything I had done for her. "We will keep in touch," she vowed. "This is not goodbye."

"I hope so, Madame," was all I could manage.

* * *

Patrick was late—again, another evening of wishing he'd materialize in front of me. When he finally appeared, sweaty from one of his pickup basketball games but full of energy, he greeted me breezily with "Hi! How was your day?"

"I lost my job."

"You what?"

"Irene's taking Gabrielle to France. She told me to cancel the show, cancel the studio appointments. I get to preside over the death of *Cooking with Irene.*"

He looked stunned. After a long silence, he asked, "What will you do?"

"Without a job? I guess I'll have to go back to Texas." Was I being honest or was I wrangling for him to pull me out of this swamp I'd fallen into? Offer to let me live with him so I didn't have to pay rent? What did I really want? I didn't know myself, and Lord knows what Patrick thought.

"Did you ever find out about the show's financing?"

I thought that was definitely an irrelevant thing to ask about at this moment. "Not really. Best I can figure is Lake Michigan Productions was a shell—it was only Howard. Maybe he used it for tax purposes, maybe not. But he paid the studio, and the network paid him. He paid my salary and covered the show credit card he gave me. John Wilson could probably verify this, if he'd really dig into the files in his office."

"So what happens to the show depends on the network."

I could almost see the wheels going around in his head.

"Tomorrow, you call the network and explain what happened. Might as well start at the top." Only then did he wrap his arms around me and whisper, "Henny, you're not going back to Texas. I promise."

I really did love that man.

＊ ＊ ＊

Next morning I stalled, afraid to take that first big step. It was Saturday, and I convinced myself I'd have to wait until Monday. On his way to the university, Patrick stuck his head in and when I explained my weekend logic to him, said sternly, "Call today, Henny."

So I screwed up my courage. Bob Thorne not only was in on a Saturday morning, but he took the call right away and gave me no time for any explanation. "I'm afraid Mrs. Foxglove's qualifications don't work. We've been billing her as a graduate of Le Cordon Bleu. We will have to cancel the show."

Haltingly, I replied that it wasn't a problem. Mrs. Foxglove was leaving for France and would not be available for tapings. I assured him I understood and thanked him for whatever and got ready to disconnect and have a good cry.

"Wait a minute," he said. "Since this came up, I've looked at some of the shows. Caught a couple where you did the intro and sign-off. You're much more of a natural than she is. Where did you do your culinary training?"

"In my mother's kitchen," I replied.

He laughed aloud, a hearty sound that almost but not quite soothed my nerves. Then he was quiet so long that my nerves ratcheted up again. I waited.

"I think it would work," he said.

What? What would work? What was he talking about? "Pardon me?"

"Your own show," he said. "We'll play up your amateur cook status. We need to attract younger people who are in the kitchen these days. I think they'll identify with you more than someone from Cordon whatever. We can produce it in our studios here. Might even call it *Recipes from My Mom's Kitchen.*"

I pinched myself. "Would you repeat that?"

He did but I barely heard what he was saying about contracts and salary—I gathered it would be an improvement. And did he really say I'd have an assistant? And he wanted two shows a week. My mind spun. How many of the recipes I already had could I use? What would I wear? Denim, of course. But no toque.

Dimly, I heard him ask me to give him a few days to work things out and set up a schedule. Could I come to the network offices on Wednesday?

Of course I could! The offices were on the near North Side, easily reached by bus. No more long ride to North Clarendon. No more saving Irene.

And that is how I came to have my own television cooking show. Granted, it was a far cry from the *Today* show, but it was a step up the ladder.

And I had the best guy in the world. Life was good.

Bon Voyage, Irene!

Some of Irene's Favorite Forty recipes

Irene's Reluctant Hamburger Stroganoff

Stroganoff is a classy dish, the kind of dinner you serve by candlelight with good red wine, on Valentine's Day . . . or as a special family treat. But there have been two classic ways to do it: with beef tenderloin, which cooks quickly and is tender, or with a cheaper cut, like beef tips, which requires all day in the crockpot. Irene reluctantly made it with hamburger, though she claimed it was awful. Most people like it.

2 lbs. ground sirloin

½ cup flour

1 tsp. salt

½ tsp. pepper

4 Tbsp. butter, divided

½ cup finely diced onion

½ lb. mushrooms, cleaned and sliced

2 cups beef stock

1 lb. egg noodles

1 cup sour cream

3 Tbsp. tomato paste

1 tsp. Worcestershire sauce

1 lb. egg noodles

Brown ground meat in 2 Tbsp. butter; if necessary, brown in batches. Stir in flour, salt, and pepper. Remove meat from skillet. Brown onion in remaining 2 Tbsp. butter (you may not need all the butter if the ground meat leaves enough grease in the skillet). When onion is translucent, add mushrooms and sauté until nicely wilted. Add beef stock and bring to slight boil, cooking until sauce thickens. Remove the pan from your hot plate.

Separately, mix sour cream, tomato paste, and Worcestershire sauce. Return meat to burner and heat. Stir a spoonful of hot beef mixture into the sour cream, and then stir the whole thing back into the meat. Do not let mixture boil. If it boils, the cream will curdle. Stir to warm the sour cream mixture and mix thoroughly, and then stir in the noodles. Noodles may be served individually, with sauce ladled on top, but stirred together the dish stays warm longer. Serve immediately.

Serves six; may be halved easily. A green salad makes a good accompaniment. Use leftovers within two or three days, and do not boil when reheating.

Irene's Wine Casserole (Sloppy Joe)

1 lb. ground beef

1 15-oz. can of beans (any kind you want), rinsed and drained

½ cup chopped onion

½ cup diced celery

2 Tbsp. bacon drippings

¼ cup ketchup

1½ Tbsp. Worcestershire sauce

Dash of Tabasco

1 tsp. salt

$1/_8$ tsp. pepper

¼ tsp. oregano

¼ cup dry red wine

1 Tbsp. A-1 sauce

Cook onion in bacon drippings. Add beef and brown. Add remaining ingredients and simmer 20 to 30 minutes. Serve in bowls or, for Sloppy Joe, on toasted buns.

Irene's Shrimp Victoria

½ cup onion, diced

1 stick butter

2 lbs. shrimp, shelled, cleaned, and cooked

1 lb. mushrooms, sliced

2 Tbsp. flour

1 tsp. salt

Pinch of pepper

2 cups sour cream, more if needed

Rice or noodles

Sauté onion in butter until translucent. Add mushrooms and cook two minutes. Add shrimp and cook four minutes, stirring.

Sprinkle flour, salt, and pepper over mixture, stirring to incorporate thoroughly.

Just before serving, stir in sour cream. Do not let it boil.

Serve over rice or noodles. Serves four. Good with a green salad.

Croque Madame

For the béchamel sauce:

5 Tbsp. butter

¼ cup flour

4 cups milk

2 tsp. salt

$1/_3$ tsp. nutmeg

For the sandwich:

8 slices country-style bread

6 oz. sliced ham, preferably French

3 oz. Gruyere (or Emmental)

Dijon mustard (optional)

To make the sauce:

Melt butter in skillet; stir in flour and cook, stirring, until flour begins to turn golden. Gradually whisk in milk (*you may want more or less*). Sauce will thicken. Cook, stirring frequently, for five minutes or more. Taste to be sure flour is no longer gritty.

To make the sandwich:

Toast bread lightly.

Coat one side of four slices with béchamel sauce, being sure to spread it to the edges. Layer ham and cheese. Coat one side of remaining pieces of bread with sauce (or you may choose to use good Dijon mustard). Put sandwiches together and spread tops with more béchamel. Top with a bit of grated cheese.

Bake in moderate oven until cheese melts. Change oven setting to broil to finish the sandwiches, watching carefully that they don't burn.

You have just made Croque Monsieur. Irene likes to turn it into Croque Madame by topping each sandwich with a sunny-side up fried egg.

Irene's Coquille St. Jacques (scallops in a cream sauce)

This company-style dish is traditionally served in a shell-shaped dish with mashed potatoes piped decoratively around the edge. Irene prefers to use individual gratin dishes with a bread crumb topping.

For the scallops:

12 large sea scallops (*count 3 scallops per serving*)

3 Tbsp. butter

1 shallot, minced

3 Tbsp. white wine

¾ cup crème fraiche

1 Tbsp. minced parsley

Salt and pepper

For the crumb topping:

1 ½ cups crustless white bread crumbs or panko

¼ cup minced parsley

5 oz. Gruyere, grated

¼ cup olive oil

Directions:

Pat scallops dry with paper towel and refrigerate, uncovered, for one hour to dry them further. Meanwhile, mince the shallot. Melt butter in skillet and sauté shallot.

Add scallops to skillet and cook until they lose their translucence and are white. Do not overcook, for it makes them rubbery. Cook, remove from skillet, and cover to keep them warm.

Deglaze the skillet with white wine, scraping browned bits off the bottom of the pan. Let wine boil gently until reduced by half. Add crème fraiche. Return scallops to pan just to mix; do not cook further.

Make the topping by mixing crumbs, parsley, and cheese. Stir in olive oil, making sure mixture is thoroughly moistened.

Butter four gratin dishes and divide scallop mixture into them. Cover with crumb mixture. Bake at 350° until scallops are just warmed through and topping is browned.

Made in the USA
Coppell, TX
27 January 2022

72387917R00121